What Gloria Wants

WHAT GLORIA WANTS

Sarah Withrow

GROUNDWOOD BOOKS
HOUSE OF ANANSI PRESS
TORONTO BERKELEY

Groundwood Books / House of Anansi Press
110 Spadina Avenue, Suite 801, Toronto, Ontario M5V 2K4
Distributed in the USA by Publishers Group West
1700 Fourth Street, Berkeley, CA 94710

We acknowledge for their financial support of our publishing program the
Canada Council for the Arts, the Government of Canada through the Book
Publishing Industry Development Program (BPIDP) and the
Ontario Arts Council.

ONTARIO ARTS COUNCIL
CONSEIL DES ARTS DE L'ONTARIO

Library and Archives Canada Cataloging in Publication
Withrow, Sarah
What Gloria wants / by Sarah Withrow.
ISBN-13: 978-0-88899-628-2 (bound).–
ISBN-10: 0-88899-628-4 (bound).–
ISBN-13: 978-0-88899-692-3 (pbk.).–
ISBN-10: 0-88899-692-6 (pbk.)
I. Title.
PS8595.I8455W43 2005   jC813'.54   C2005-902994-3

Printed and bound in Canada

For Mom

Second Good

━━━

I point to the empty bowl, and Shawna shakes in six chips.

"More," I tell her.

"Don't be a moo," she says. "Fat chicks don't get boyfriends, Glor."

"I don't care."

"But you have to care." She takes the bowl away from me. "How are we supposed to be double-date best friends with truly hot boyfriends if you become a fat chick?"

Shawna has all these plans for us double-dating in high school. They're kind of terrifying, like R-rated Olsen twins fantasies. She'll get a guy who's complicated and secretly studly (meaning he wears glasses), and he'll end up inventing something worth billions of dollars, like an environmentally friendly material that acts like breathable leather. And I'm supposed to find a guy – and this is pure Shawna – who's a hot dancer who likes to read all night. And he'll write a book that he'll promote through dancing and we'll live in New York, which, she says, is the only city you can be a rich non-ballet dancer in.

I don't even know what I want to do tomorrow, and Shawna's already got it all figured out until we're practically dead. She even had it that we both retire to Fiji with our husbands where we'd play with our grandchildren on the beach. I told her Fiji might be too hot for me, and she actually got mad. Two days later, out of the blue, she announced that we can retire to the mountains instead and play with our grandchildren by a pool.

The only thing I really like about Shawna's plans is that they always include me.

"Maybe I'll meet a guy who'll love me for my mind," I tell her and make a dive for the chip bowl. She jerks it away and stuffs half of what's in there in her tiny face.

"I'm saving you," she sputters through the crumbs. I grab the bag and she tries to wrestle it from me, but she can hardly breathe through her mouthful of chips and I'm way bigger than her and have superior strength, so it's no use.

I only feel big next to her because she's so small. We used to be the same size, but I've been growing. A lot.

"I don't need saving," I say. She acts like I don't know that she's the pretty one, the one who went skinny-dipping at camp and got caught kissing Justin Hellbrig behind the washroom near the bumper cars at Lake Ontario Park.

"Take it easy, Glor. I was just kidding. Actually, go right ahead. Eat the whole bowl. I don't need the competition. Hey, that's not a bad plan. We should put chips in all the girls' lockers. Then they all bulk up, and me and you will rule the school."

"Or the guys learn to love big girls," I point out.

"Yeah, like you really believe that will happen." She looks at the chips in my hand.

I put one in my mouth and one back in the bowl.

She pours the rest of the bag into the bowl, takes a handful and passes the bowl to me.

"You've got nothing to worry about," she says, like she's reading my mind. "I bet you even get a guy before I do."

"You are such a liar," I say.

"I'm serious, Glor. You've got the whole package. You're smart, you're nice, you're pretty, and you're growing a set of killer boobs," she smiles. I pull a pillow off the couch and throw it at her.

"Shut up." It's all I can think of to say as I feel myself blush three flesh tones. I've been wearing a B-cup bra since the summer, but I tried on Mom's C-cup in the laundry room and it does fit better. I'm not going to tell Shawna, though. It's one thing for her to say that about me. It's another for her to know it as a fact of life. And if she knows it and doesn't like it…that equals trouble.

Besides, it doesn't matter how good a package you are, you still eventually have to say something to the guy, right? I'm not shy in real life, but when it comes to certain guys, I go all weird. Like when I spent all night making cookies in Shawna's kitchen because I couldn't be in the same room as Gordon Peakes at her birthday party. I was so relieved when he moved to Cornwall so that I didn't have to live in fear of seeing him in the hall.

I never tell Shawna if I like a guy, because she'd make me talk to him or, worse, she'd talk to him for me. I don't know why I'm so like that. Mom says it's probably because it's all women in my family — her, me and my not-so-little sister, Hazel. And Dad, but he doesn't count.

I think it's because my eyes are allergic to the eyes of boys I like. Any time they look at me, I have to look away. I don't like it when I catch them looking at me. It makes me feel like I'm suddenly in some kind of glass bubble. A couple of times it was like I could feel a guy liking me with his eyes. But how can a guy like me when I haven't said a single word to him?

I'm glad Shawna has high school all figured out, because my plan is to stand behind her for the next four years.

"We absolutely have to stop eating these," Shawna says and takes the bowl and throws the rest of the chips in the garbage.

•

"The black dress is elegant, but gold is only fitting for the goddess I've become."

Shawna has three Barbies. Good is the one with the long blonde hair. Second Good also has long blonde hair but has a wire poking out of her foot, and Ugly Naked has her hair all cut off and green magic marker on her face. We use Ugly Naked to be the boyfriend. Shawna always gets Good and I always get Second Good. We fight over which one of us gets to be escorted by Ugly Naked. We call this the man shortage argument.

I am almost fourteen and really too old to be playing with dolls, but it's fun to have the Barbies be really evil on their pretend dates. We get them to kick each other in the head, commit ax murders on fashion models, visit crack houses, be strippers at fancy-ass rich clubs, smoke cigarillos and have sex with Ugly Naked. They have slutty plastic Barbie sex about as often as they go to the pretend washroom to smoke big joints, snort cocaine or slap each other across the face for being uppity. They do it with Ugly Naked five times a pretend night. Sometimes more.

Good and Second Good Barbie are very, very bad girls. But only Good ever gets to wear the gold dress.

"Can Second Good wear the gold dress on my birthday?" I ask. I know I let Shawna be the boss of me. It works out, though. I may owe her for making decisions and figuring things out, but she owes me for letting her lead. It's not often I make a special request, like with the gold dress.

I've never seen what it looks like on Second Good Barbie and tomorrow is my birthday and I think it's time Second Good got a taste of the Good Life.

Shawna considers my request from her perch on her bed, which is so huge it makes her look like a little doll herself.

"What kind of evil mistress of birthday wrecking do you take me for? Of course Second can wear the gold dress tomorrow."

"And get Ugly Naked to dance with her all night at the Luscious-Land Night Club?"

"Of course. Gloria gets what Gloria wants on her birthday. That's the rule. Only…"

"Only what?" I am reading the look on my best

friend's face. It is saying, "I don't want to be without a date at Luscious-Land on Gloria's birthday. I can be gracious and lend her the gold dress, but I do not think I can bear to be without a date." She rolls over on her bed and holds Ugly Naked over her head.

"If only we had another Ugly Naked," she says. I can feel a serious man shortage argument coming on, and I know it's going to be a sucky birthday if we can't find Shawna a date. A date for her doll, I mean.

"We could split Ugly Naked in two," I say. Shawna, I can tell, likes the idea.

"Let's do it like a wishbone. You take a leg and I'll take a leg and whoever gets the most of it gets her wish."

I don't know what to wish for. It seems like this is an opportunity for some real major wish because it's special and it's about breaking Ugly Naked and about turning fourteen and starting high school and...

I know what I want.

"Okay," I say and grab a plastic leg. Shawna counts to three and we pull. It's harder than I thought it would be to tear Ugly Naked apart. I lean back and Shawna leans back. I can't believe how hard she's trying to win the wish when it's my birthday tomorrow. It's not like I ask for much.

I hear a snap and Ugly Naked's leg comes off in my hand. I fall back onto Shawna's plush green carpet. I look at the flesh-colored piece of plastic in my hand and bend it at the knee. Shawna holds the rest of Ugly Naked over her head in victory.

"What did you wish for?" I ask.

"If I tell it might not come true. How about you?"

"I'm not telling either," I say. Shawna rolls her eyes and I get annoyed at myself for being sucky over losing the wishbone break. "Fine. I wished for a boyfriend."

Shawna grins and throws me Ugly Naked.

"Here you go. Your wish is granted."

I let the one-legged Ugly Naked lie face down on the floor by the stack of magazines we use as Luscious-Land's back alley where the Barbies have sex.

"I think I'd rather date Leggy, actually." I hold the leg up. I hold it like it's a whole doll and walk it across the top of the stack of magazines and have it jump around a few times like a really hot dancer. "He seems flexible and athletic."

I'm reading my best friend's face and it's saying, "I want Leggy, the plastic leg boyfriend."

That's my one for-sure talent. I know how to make Shawna want what I have. I don't know if I can count it as a real talent, though, because basically, Shawna wants everything.

Marc Le Clare (Maybe)
Looks at Me

Fast forward to the second week of grade nine. I'm alone in the cafeteria because Shawna picked drama instead of art, so our class schedules don't match and now I don't have anyone to eat with on Tuesdays and Thursdays.

Today I'm sitting at the back of the cafeteria, so that I can keep track of the action I'm not participating in and the players I'm not speaking to, so that I can report back to Shawna. Most of the grade nines at Earl Secondary came from Rideau School, while only a few, like me and Shawna, came from Central. Most of the kids from Central went to West Tech, but Earl has a better academic reputation. The Rideau kids are big and loud and look like they come from families that eat pizza for dinner every night.

I like eating with Shawna but, man, can that girl

talk. Like yesterday she had to tell me what kind of underwear every girl in her gym class wears: elastic, color, cut, material. She even talked about how Rachel Pepper's gotch rolled up when she took them off to put on her bathing suit. I did not need that picture in my head. According to Shawna, the right kind of underwear is black with two little cloth flowers sewn to the corners at the hip bones, which are supposed to be sticking out.

I'm wearing my Sunday day-of-the-week underwear from the set Mom bought when I was twelve. It's really tight. My new ones are all in the pile of laundry at the bottom of the basement stairs. Mom says, "You're welcome to do the laundry, darling," but I'm not setting a laundry precedent like I accidentally did with mowing the lawn. Let Hazel get suckered this time.

A blob of tuna lands splat on my favorite Catwoman T-shirt.

I'm trying to stop the tuna from falling out of my sandwich when I catch Marc Le Clare looking in my direction.

Who is he looking at? I look around. Then I check Marc again and he's not looking at me anymore. Not like he *was* looking at me.

Shawna thinks he's cute. She rates him a nine minus, which is her highest score (except for Orlando Bloom, who gets ten plus). She's already found out that Marc used to have a girlfriend but that she moved out west. He's got good teeth, slightly curly dark hair, dimples, blue eyes and nice long muscular body sides. This Rideau girl, Tina, told Shawna that all the girls at her old school wanted to go out with him because of his dimples and muscular sides, but that his ex-girlfriend, Serena, was the only one who did. And Tina also told Shawna that Marc's best friend, Hamish (who Shawna rates a "slight seven"), got lost in the woods camping when he was ten and his parents didn't tell the park ranger until three o'clock in the morning. They found him the next day asleep in a rotten tree and, Tina told Shawna, he had his thumb in his mouth when they found him.

Hamish is supposed to be a total jerk and supposedly tortured Marc's girlfriend, Serena, with crank calls.

Shawna's theory is that Hamish thinks he's protecting Marc when really Hamish is just overcompensating because he's the one who really feels like he needs protection because he's got idiot parents. Tina, the girl Shawna found all this out from, still thinks Hamish is a first-class jerk. He looks like a first-class jerk to me in the way he bounces on his legs when he walks and never takes off his black leather jacket, which is obviously too big for his scrawny body. I personally would rate him a six at best — if I played the rate game, which I don't because it's demeaning.

Shawna thinks she's the expert on guys just because she made out with Justin Hellbrig in grade seven and then went skinny-dipping with Lawrence at rich-kid sleepover horse camp. It wasn't just him and her alone swimming, though. It was a whole group of them, but you wouldn't know it from the way she talks about "when Lawrence threw me in the lake." Apparently his hoo-ha touched her leg while they were wrestling on the dock.

Shawna'll probably make Marc be her boyfriend and I'll end up eating lunch alone every single day. Pretending I don't care. Pretending to love every second of the shy-girl hell I'll be in.

Just like I'm doing right now, listening to myself chew.

I pick off the slimy ends of lettuce hanging out the side of my sandwich, and the tuna flops out onto the table. I start picking up the tuna and look over at Marc. He turns his head away fast. Then Hamish looks at me through the dirty blond hair hanging in front of his face, and I drop my eyes.

My face goes hot as I stare at the destroyed tuna sandwich and try to think what to feel.

•

I wait in the hall by Shawna's locker after school, sitting on my books so my bum won't get cold. I have more than enough homework to keep my butt off the ground. Shawna comes down the hall with that girl, Tina, the one who tells her about the kids who came from Rideau. Tina always wears hip-huggers, but she kind of looks like she's getting squeezed out of them.

Tina waves.

"Hi." She's chewing on a straw and shifting from one foot to the other like she has to go to the washroom.

"I've got ten hours' worth of crud," I announce. Shawna opens her locker and starts fussing with her stuff. She always takes forever doing nothing.

"French and more French," Shawna says. "I'm not doing the math. Nobody can make me. English I'll do, but I'm going to whine the entire time. Did she say Act One for you guys, too?" I nod. "A whole act in one night? I was going to sew pink things on my pansy shirt."

"They give us so much homework," says Tina, wanting in. She's still shuffling.

"Where's your locker?" I ask her.

"I don't know," she says, looking down the hall. "They gave me one, but I can't find it. I think it's in the basement, but, anyway, I can never work those locks. I just carry everything around. It makes it so heavy, but it's good exercise." She trails off, sighs and bites her straw. Her ponytails are lopsided and her belly sticks out over her pants. She reminds me of the Easter Bunny.

I look up at Shawna.

"So, your house?" I ask her.

"Yeah," says Tina. Shawna looks down at me, seeing if it's okay for Tina to come, since Tina obviously thinks she's coming.

"We'll act out Act One. Tina can be Caesar," I offer, to show I'm not jealous of Tina, which I'm not.

"Isn't he a guy?" Tina asks.

"It's all guys," Shawna explains. "Except Portia. I'm Portia. Called it."

She's almost got herself together. Shawna likes to have people wait for her. I don't mind. Waiting can be very peaceful. Unless you shuffle like Tina. Then it's exercise. My bum is numb.

"You be Portia, Tina will be Caesar and I'll be Marc — "

And then, as if God heard me, Marc Le Clare comes strolling down the hall with Hamish, the muscular edges of his long sides showing through his red T-shirt.

My heart burps.

"Hi," Marc says as he breezes by. Tina and Shawna watch him pass and then turn to stare at me. I pick at a spot of dried tuna on my T-shirt.

"…I'll be Marc Anthony," I say, thinking how well I just recovered. "He has the best speech."

"He has the best something," Tina says, staring down the hall at Marc with big dreamy eyes, straw hanging out the side of her mouth.

"Did he just say hi to you?" says Shawna, like she's accusing me of something.

"What?" I try to sound oblivious. "I thought he was talking to Tina. You know him from Rideau, right?"

"I know him. Like I know who he is and he knows who I am because we went to the same school and I knew his old girlfriend, Serena, but I don't know him, know him."

I'm glad I didn't say anything to Shawna about Marc maybe looking at me at lunch. Stomach-churning action tells me he really might have been saying hi to me.

He doesn't know he can't do that.

Wait.

Why can't he do that?

•

We go to Shawna's and use the Barbies to act out the first act of Julius Caesar. Tina plays Caesar with Ugly Naked and breaks us up when she pants, "Et, *TOOO*, Brutay?" Like Caesar was Darth Vader. Then

Shawna/Brutus/Good stabs Ugly Naked a few thousand more times than necessary, and then Dad calls for me to come home for dinner and won't believe that I am busy doing homework because there is too much giggling in the background.

The Problem with My Face

My parents think that eating dinner with their kids every night is what makes them good parents. I could be shooting heroin in the back alley and they wouldn't care as long as I was home in time to set the table.

Tonight we're having stuffed green peppers and stuffed mushrooms.

"It looks like alien food," Hazel complains, looking down at the huge portobello mushroom cap topped with cheese beside the mushy green pepper sitting in a pool of its own green juice.

"You girls are welcome to cook any time," Mom says, cutting into her mushroom cap and making it leak black mushroom juice onto the orange plate.

"It does look a little like surrealist art, Leila," Dad says, then checks Mom's face, which is sometimes hard to pick out when she lets her bushy dark hair swing forward. "In the best possible way, of course."

During dinner we learn that Dad misses having co-workers, that Mom would trade with him any day of the week and that Hazel's best friend, Lisa, has been grounded because she called her mother a whore when she found out her mom is pregnant by her mom's new boyfriend.

Dad laughs when Hazel tells about Lisa. Mom gives him the evil eye.

I tell about Julius Caesar with Barbies and about Tina wearing hip-huggers that don't fit. Mom thinks I'm being rude to Tina by even talking about her hips, but Hazel defends me, saying, "It's not Tina's fault she's wearing the wrong pants. It's society's fault. Just because Gloria noticed doesn't make her rude, Mom."

Dad agrees that society makes some girls wear bad pants. Then Mom laughs and Dad tries to give her the evil eye.

We don't have dessert.

Me and Hazel go upstairs and I lock myself in the bathroom so she can't bug me.

I kneel on the toilet seat and examine my face in the mirror. I still haven't told anyone about Marc Le Clare maybe looking at me. That could have been accidental at lunch. I don't think so. He could have been saying hi to Tina after school today, too. But I think he was saying it to me. He just made a mistake, that's all. He just didn't get that good a look at me.

If he had, he would have noticed how my eyes are plain brown and two different sizes and shapes. One is more round and the other more squinty and they both kind of point into my nose. My nostrils are also two different sizes. One is twice the size of the other and you can tell it easily when I smile because my smile is also lop-sided so that only half of my teeth show. I've tried to even it out by smiling with my whole mouth, but then my smile looks all forced and fake.

That's the main problem with my face. It's crooked. It wouldn't be so bad if I didn't smile, but I can't help it.

If Marc was only looking at one side of my face or the other, I might look kind of pretty. Sometimes I imagine I'm one of those girls in the back line of the dancers in a black-and-white movie musical, because my hair crosses my forehead with a little wave like the women used to have back in those movies. I'd be in the back line because I need the head of the woman in front of me to hide my thighs. Also, the costume would have lots of feathers.

Shawna told me the other day that my hair looks truly great now, although I don't see what's good about it now that wasn't good about it before this summer. It's the same hair, basically. Maybe it's the right thickness, or maybe it looks good from the back.

I can't see my back and I won't be held responsible for what it looks like. It's enough to have to worry about the front of myself. I turn to the side in the mirror.

I always wished for breasts that were big enough that they would hold the material of my shirt out like a little tent. I didn't think I'd end up with the Big Top. I wish I could unwish my breasts because they're all floppy and gross and don't look anything like the ones we saw in Shawna's brother's *Playboys*. My hips are really wide, too. There's no way my hip bones would poke out enough to hold up tiny flowers on little black underwear. And I wouldn't even dream of wearing hip-huggers.

My stomach isn't bad, but my innie bellybutton is so deep Shawna says it has its own echo.

I smile lop-sided at the mirror and try to see what a guy might see. I try to see myself as a stranger, a girl across a room at a party. If I walked in and saw Gloria Nunes, would I think she was pretty?

I smile again with my whole mouth, catch my own eye and ruin the whole thing.

That's the other problem with my face. Anyone can tell what I'm thinking at any second because I never learned how to be truly cool in my expressions. I think the crookedness makes it harder to not show my feelings.

Tomorrow I have to remember to keep my head down when I see Marc, so he can't see how surprised I am that he might like me. If I look at him and he sees me, and I see him seeing me, I'll be in a glass bubble all day.

I can't really like him anyway. I haven't even talked to him yet. And I don't want to get in a man shortage argument with Shawna about him. Just because he's good-looking...What kind of talent does that take?

When I go to our room Hazel's waiting for me with the brush, picking her nose and reading a magazine.

"Rapunzel?" she asks. She's eleven. Sometimes she looks older, sometimes she looks younger. My hair is all right, but Hazel's is red. She is going to be so hot when she gets older. She knows it, too. Hazel is the kind of girl who always wears the right pants.

I sit behind her on her bed, gather up her hair and brush it all over on one side of her head.

"I'm going to make you crooked," I tell her. "Do you think the prince will mind?"

But she's busy reading and picking her nose again and doesn't answer me.

•

The next morning, I wait for Shawna at the corner near Victoria Park. Maybe Marc was looking at me because my face is crooked. I need for her to honestly tell me if my face is freakishly crooked.

She's with Tina.

Shawna and Tina make their way down the street toward me. Is this going to happen every day? When they reach me, they are so busy talking that they hardly notice me, and I have to wait for a break in their conversation about cellphones before I can work my way in.

"Do you live around here?" I ask Tina, who darts a look at Shawna before answering.

"Not really, but I'm going for a walk before school in the mornings because I need the exercise. Shawna said I could walk to her house if I wanted, which is really great because I needed a place to walk to, because before I just went around the block and that wasn't far enough for me to lose weight. I was losing about four calories walking around the block. That's not even a bite of ham. I hope it's all right," she adds at the end, which shows she knows it's really not.

"Why wouldn't it be all right?" Shawna says. I try to smile with my whole mouth so that I won't look lopsided and I know, right away, that she sees I'm put out.

Then she smiles to show me that she meant for me

to be put out and I know, right away, that she's jealous because Marc said hi to me yesterday.

I love how she's allowed to get all jealous over something that isn't even my fault and I'm supposed to understand. But if I say one thing about how lucky she is about having her own room with a canopy bed, or how good she looks in jeans because she has boy hips, then she gets to say, "Get over it."

I love how every problem there's ever been between us is my problem.

•

I make a point of sitting beside Vanessa in science class because Mr. Rokosh said that we were going to partner up starting today and Tina says that Vanessa won the science fair at Rideau. I'm the best at history. Last year, anyway. The only real bonus of being best at something is that then you don't have to worry about having to get better at it, although now I have to worry about one of the kids from Rideau maybe being better than me.

Vanessa smiles at me, so I know she's good with me sitting here. Too bad we don't get history partners. Me and Shawna have that class together. She knows I'm best in history and if we were partners, I'd get to be the boss for once.

I'm daydreaming about bossing Shawna while Mr. Rokosh explains about the partners.

Suddenly, everyone is groaning. I look around, trying to figure out what's going on.

"This is so stupid," Vanessa says, bending over her notebook. She writes down her name and tears out the page. Mr. Rokosh is wandering around the room gathering scraps of paper in a Maple Leafs hockey toque.

"What's this for?" I ask as Mr. Rokosh makes his way toward us.

"Please, let me get you," Vanessa says as she puts her name in the hat. Mr. Rokosh shakes the toque for me to drop my name in. I try to make it so it's close to Vanessa's when it goes in.

When Mr. Rokosh gets to the front of the class, he makes a big show of shaking the toque. He even puts it on with the names in it and shakes his head like he's listening to heavy metal music. Nobody laughs.

Finally he takes it off and pulls out a name. It's not mine. He matches it with another, not mine. He keeps on.

Vanessa gets Marta, and breathes a sigh of relief, but with both of them gone, the only person left for me to hope to get is…Marc. And I can't want that. I can't even secretly want it, because it will show on my face.

"Mr. Marc Le Clare," Mr. Rokosh calls out. I pinch

the tip of my pinky finger so that I'll look like I'm in pain. "You're with Wyatt." I store the info for Shawna and let my breath out slowly so Vanessa won't notice I was holding it.

There's only five of us left. Maybe I won't get a partner and Mr. Rokosh will let me go with Vanessa and Marta.

"Hamish," Mr. Rokosh calls out. "You're with…" He reaches in. "Gloria Nunes."

"Oh, my God," I mumble. Vanessa pats me on the back. I look over my shoulder and Hamish is glaring at me with his arms crossed, like it's my fault. Beside him, Marc whispers something in his ear. Hamish nods and looks sideways at me. He raises a finger up.

I think that's Hamish for a wave.

Mr. Rokosh says for us to sit with our partners and decide which experiments we will do for the Fluids and Pressures module. The fluids in my brain put pressure on my skull as Vanessa gets up and goes to sit with Marta.

"Good luck," she says.

"You, too," I tell her. And it's like we've been forever best friends in how much it hurts to watch her walk across the room away from me, but I focus hard on her footsteps because I don't want to get to the next minute.

It's no use. I feel Hamish plunk himself down beside

me. His legs scrunch up against the lab counter and I sense him slouch back on his stool. I close my eyes and turn my head. When I open them again, he's sitting there, flicking the end of his pen against his teeth and shifting the shape of his mouth to change the pitch of the sound it makes.

"I guess we're partners," I say and hold out my hand for him to shake. He pulls my finger and smiles through his pen-rattling mouth. Then he stops and lets his bony hands flop by his sides.

"Lucky you," he says and sits up, grabbing the paper with the experiment list from in front of me. "I know my choices. Now, you choose, see? Then if your choices are the same as mine, no problem. If one's different, no problem. If two are different, we discuss. If three are different, problem. Go." He shoves the paper back, weaves his fingers together and rests them on his stomach.

I look down at the paper and then over at Vanessa and Marta, busy chatting over the different options. Go? At least he's efficient. I study the paper.

"Two, five and eight," I say and slide the paper across the desk to him. "Problem?"

He picks the paper up again and examines my choices. I don't think he actually did have any picked. He looks at the paper and then to the back of the room.

He looks at the paper again and then over at the clock.

I keep my head down, waiting to see if he'll decide he wants to have a problem with me or not. Is this what it's going to be like all term?

Is it too early to ask Mr. Rokosh if we can change partners?

I hear a laugh from across the class. Hamish turns his head, and I follow. Marc is watching him. Us.

"Shut up," Hamish says and then notices Mr. Rokosh looking our way. He looks at me. "What a retard," he says.

"I thought you two were best friends."

"I'm best friends with a retard, then." He starts flicking his pen in his mouth again. "I'm good with your choices," he mumbles, pointing at the paper.

"No problem?" I ask, trying to lighten things up. We've still got twelve minutes to kill before the bell rings.

"Disappointed?" he asks. I shake my head. "I bet," he mutters under his breath.

During the next eleven minutes and twenty-two seconds, Hamish gives Marc the finger fourteen times while I reread the list of experiments and doodle circles around numbers two, five and eight.

•

All during art, I do pen-and-ink cross-hatched drawings of martello towers and think about how I have to spend all term with Hamish's attitude. "Disappointed?" he says. "I bet," he says. His sarcasm sticks in my head like maple syrup, gooing up everything.

"You're tearing the paper," says Tiziano, who sits beside me. He's drawing rabbits. He told me he's going to give the picture to his grandmother. She fell down the basement stairs during a Labor Day barbecue. He told me his aunt brought a plate of hamburgers to the waiting room at the hospital.

"She knew we were hungry. No sense letting it go to waste," he said, like he was arguing with me, even though I hadn't said anything about it. I can hear him breathing over his page, trying to get the rabbit eyes right for his grandma.

I pick my page up and, sure enough, there are ink scratches on the table. I wave the thing at Tiz to show him he was right.

"You're allowed to take your time, you know," he says. "Ever hear anyone say Michelangelo was a fast artist?"

The Fast Artist

It's my job to save the seats in the cafeteria because I'm the only one who brings her lunch, because my family has been poor ever since Dad bought the big-ass computer that he's not making any money off of and won't let us use. He keeps talking about the learning curve and saying how it will pay off big time once he taps the hidden market. I just wish he would stop trying to make it up to me and Hazel by experimenting with our sandwich fillings. Today it's honey mustard and peanut butter on whole grain with lettuce. I sniff the boiled-vegetable-and-fried air wafting from the cafeteria lineup and pray that Shawna comes back with something shareable.

She's paying for her food now, with Tina right behind her.

"I'm only going to eat seven of them. No. Twelve.

I'm only going to eat twelve fries," says Tina, sitting down. "Just enough to get rid of the craving and then you guys have to eat the rest so that they don't accidentally make it into my mouth."

"How can you eat accidentally?" I ask.

"You'll see," Tina says seriously. Shawna laughs way too loudly and plunks her tray down next to Tina's. Tina looks at me like, "What's up with her?" and I begin to suspect that I could secretly like Tina — if she weren't standing next to Shawna every single time I see her. Doesn't she have any friends of her own?

Shawna's got tomato soup. Soup's not a sharing food.

"Soooo," says Shawna, poking her nose in the air. "Marta told me that you and Hamish are science partners. Think you can arrange to study with him and Marc?"

Tina raises her eyebrows and stuffs three fries in her mouth. "You got Hamish?" she says with her mouth full. I grab a fry off her tray, before the accidental eating shifts into full gear. I nod and stare at Shawna.

I don't know what to say. One look at her tells me she's spent geography class turning this names-from-a-hat twist of fate into a date with her and Marc Le Clare. She's got the steps all worked out and if I don't do what she says, she'll tell the entire school about my days-of-the-week underwear.

"You should be careful with that guy," says Tina. "He stepped on a squirrel once."

"What?" we ask at the same time.

"Yeah. Last spring. You know when all the baby squirrels get born and you see so many dead animals on the road? Well, there was one on Division Street and he stepped on it. It was already dead, but still. He is mental, that Hamish. I told you about him sucking his thumb in the tree, right? Yeah. You should be careful with him in a science class. Wear your hair up."

"So he doesn't light it on fire?" I ask.

"No. Your hair would look good up. You should wear it up," Tina says, shaking a fry at my hair.

I take another one of her fries and turn to Shawna.

"I know what you are thinking and you can forget it. This is strictly a science thing. You heard Tina. He stepped on a squirrel."

"Drastic times, drastic measures," says Shawna, and I can tell from the gleam in her beady blue eyes that she's not about to give up so easily on her chance with Marc Le Clare. Her chance. That's the way she's thinking about it, even after I was the one he said hi to in the hall – no, especially because he said hi to me in the hall. "All I'm asking is that you make up an excuse to see Hamish after school at the library or something. You know, for science reasons. 'Hamish, we need to plan our experiment. Meet me outside Exit 5 after school?' That's all you have to do. I'll take it from there. You won't even have to be with him five minutes alone."

"There's no guarantee that Marc will be with him," I protest. I hate this.

"Oh, he'll be there," Tina assures Shawna. I take five of her fries, enough for her to notice. "Thanks," she says, honestly.

"Hamish called Marc a retard," I tell Shawna. I can't believe she's going to make me do this.

"So? All studs are retards," she replies. "Do it tomorrow, okay? No sense dragging our feet on this thing."

I don't want to do it. I'm going to mess it up. If she wants Marc, she should fix it herself. This is all just because he said hi to me. One word. I'm just going to tell her I'm not going to do it. Only… the words won't come out of my mouth.

Tina looks nervously at Shawna and shoves a handful of fries in her face.

"You should be careful with Hamish. He's really not nice. You can tell that, right, Gloria?"

"Yeah. What is so drastic about these times anyway? What's the rush?" I burst. Shawna is going to make me do this and I'm going to mess it up and now Tina knows and she's so excited that she's jiggling her leg under the table.

"Come on. We've talked about this, Glor. We have to set the tone for our high school years early, or else. You don't want to end up eating alone in the corner like him." Shawna waves over to a guy wiping tomato sauce off his chin and the white undershirt under his green plaid shirt. We watch him pull a gold chain from around his neck and run the paper towel down it and then look at the paper towel to see if he got anything. "If you don't want to do it just say so. I can figure out something else. It just seemed like a good opportunity, that's all. I thought we could make it so we all study together."

Now. I should tell her now that I'm not doing it.

"At your house, right?" Tina asks. Shawna's house has a sauna off the master bedroom and satellite TV.

So Shawna gets Marc and I'm supposed to fight over squirrel-boy with Tina. Or am I expected to get her a boyfriend, too?

"Yeah. We'll put on some music, I'll get some chips — "

"Or angel food cake. It's low fat," says Tina, stealing back one of the fries I took from her.

"Yeah, sure. If it happens." Shawna looks pointedly at me. She's giving me the chance to say I won't do it. "I'd do it if I were Hamish's science partner, Gloria. You have to do this for the team. You're in position. You can see that. Seriously, is it really that big a deal?"

Yes. Yes it is. Because Hamish is going to know and he's going to think it's me who wants it. And it is me who wants it and Shawna knows it, like she knows everything. She knows exactly how to play every situation to accentuate her own Good Barbieness and get whatever primo thing there is to get out of everyone.

"I didn't say it was a big deal," I hear myself say. "I'll try tomorrow, but just so you know, I'm not guaranteeing anything. You know how Hamish is, right, Tina? He is not thrilled with this science partner situation."

"Just say what I said to say. That's it. You remember, right? Meet outside Exit 5 to discuss experiment," Shawna repeats slowly. "That's it."

"Don't treat me like I'm a retard. He's going to know that's not it, Shawna. Why wouldn't we just discuss science in science class?"

"Don't get your panties in a knot. Of course he's going to know what's going on. That doesn't matter, as long as he shows up. Actually, it's better if you are obvious about it being extraneous."

Shawna's back in the driver's seat now. Why do I always give in to her?

"Extraneous?" Tina asks.

"Don't worry, Tina. Gloria knows what it means. She's one smart cookie. All A's last year. Gloria's a brainer. Don't tell anyone."

Then Shawna grabs one of the fries that I stole from Tina and bites its head off.

•

After school, I tell Shawna and Tina that I have to go straight home to look after Hazel because Dad has a late meeting. I also tell them I have to pick something up at the store before heading home so that I won't have to walk with them. I could tell that made Shawna nervous.

Let her worry about me. That's the price she pays for playing me for her puppet.

I just didn't want to talk about the whole Hamish outside Exit 5 thing all night long. I don't even care anymore. I just want Shawna's whole plan to be over and done with so that she'll get off me. The sooner she gets what she wants, the sooner things will go back to normal. I'll be the smart one and she can get us double dates. Oops. Forgot about Tina. Shawna will have to get us team dates.

Whoever. Whatever.

I pick a leaf off a bush in somebody's yard and try to peel the guts of it away from the stem.

I throw the leaf on the road.

Some other kids see me and I feel self-conscious and take an extraneous turn at the next corner, feeling my eyes fill with tears for no reason. A man is coming down the street on the other side. He's looking at me. I press both my palms to my eyes as we pass each other. I choke on a sob and feel it in the sides of my jaw.

I try to swallow to calm myself down, but the pine cone of pain in my throat won't let me. I wipe my eyes on the cuff of my sweater and take deeper breaths of cool air. I close my eyes while I walk and feel my wet lashes against the tops of my cheeks.

Why am I crying?

I accidentally step off the side of the sidewalk and go down sideways on my foot. I go a couple of more steps before deciding I really am in pain and have to sit down on the edge of the sidewalk. The gutter is full of dead leaves – red, yellow, brown and still glistening from last night's rain.

I take off my shoe and look at my ankle. I think I twisted it.

A hand swoops down and nabs my shoe.

I look up behind me. It's Hamish.

"What are you doing?" I ask. He throws the shoe from hand to hand and then sniffs it, inhaling deeply. I ignore that part and look behind him to see if anyone else is coming. "Do you live around here?"

He shakes his head and starts tossing the shoe again. I stare down at the leaves, waiting for him to give it up or, at least, say something, but he just keeps going on and on tossing the shoe.

Finally, I can't take it anymore.

"Can I have my shoe back?" I reach for it and he takes a step back. Now I'm mad. "Come on, Hamish." I twist on my bum on the sidewalk so that I'm facing him. He keeps tossing the shoe higher and higher.

I hate his stringy sideburns. I hate his scummy leather jacket and his dirty black jeans and his mussed-up shaggy hair. Most of all I hate the way he narrows his eyes and lets his tongue half hang out of his open mouth as he throws and catches my new-for-school suede sneaker.

I cross my arms on my knees and rest my head against them listening to the rhythm of the shoe toss. Throw, thump, throw, thump, throw.

"Hey, lookie what I got here for you, friend," Hamish yells. I lift my head. Oh, God. Here comes Marc. "You think it's a coincidence she's sitting three doors down from your house?" Hamish shakes the shoe at me, biting his lower lip.

Is that true?

"I twisted my ankle," I say, way too defensively. I feel the tears trying to leak out, but I order them off.

I will not cry in front of boys. And I definitely will not cry in front of Hamish, primo jerk.

Marc looks down at me, then grabs the shoe out of

mid-air as Hamish tosses it. He squats down and hands it to me.

"Are you all right?" he asks. I can't look at him, so I work on loosening the laces on the shoe. I can feel his shadow being on me, though. It makes it hard to concentrate.

"I'm fine. I was just checking my ankle. I stepped on my foot funny. Funnily. I stepped on it the wrong way."

Marc picks up my foot, forcing me to put my hands back on the sidewalk. He's touching me. Hamish is watching, as if me and Marc are on television. He thinks my twisted ankle is extraneous. He thinks I'm obvious and desperate. Tomorrow everyone will know that Hamish thinks I faked a bad foot near Marc's house to get Marc to touch me.

"It does look swollen," Marc says to him. He did think that I might be hanging around his house trying to run into him. He's the one who said hi to me.

"It's fine," I say. I tug my foot out of his grasp, put my shoe on and stand up without tying it. I step off the curb and nearly fall over again.

I will not cry.

I do my best to straighten up and manage to hobble across the street. It does hurt, but it's not too bad. I can make it home.

It hurts. It hurts a lot, but I only have to make it

to the phone booth by the convenience store and Dad will pick me up. I just need to stop for half a second.

I stop and look back at the boys. Hamish has his hands in his pockets. Marc is in the middle of the road. He's coming to get me. I shuffle faster. The ankle feels like it's a cement beach-ball of throbbing pain. I can hear Marc getting closer.

"It's fine," I call. I straighten up more and clench my hands to help my concentration. He won't stop coming.

"Stop already," he says. I want to stop now, but I can't. If Shawna hears that I twisted my ankle in front of Marc Le Clare's house…

He runs in front of me and holds out his hands to stop my shoulders.

I look at him. He knows I'm not faking. Tears come. I blink fast to soak them up. I try to move past, but Marc takes my arm and weaves it over his shoulder. I lean on him. The relief to my foot is instant.

"Thanks," I mutter.

"I live right over there. We'll put ice on it and you can call your mom, all right?"

"No," I say. He tightens his arm around me and I look at his dimples.

"Why not?" he asks. His breath smells like Skittles.

"All right." It can't be my fault. I didn't mean for this

to happen. It's like names from a hat. It doesn't mean anything. I have to go with him.

Is he holding me extraneously?

Once we've stumbled up the porch stairs, Hamish opens the screen door for us and unlocks the front door with a key from his own chain and holds it open for us.

Marc sits me down in the big leather recliner in his ultra-clean living-room and dials it into the reclining position so that I'm staring directly into Hamish's bent-over face. He winks at me and twirls the key chain around his finger.

No answer at my house. Dad must be in the bath. I leave a message and hang up. Both Marc and Hamish are sitting on the long leather couch waiting for me to report.

"No answer. Maybe I should just call a cab." I pick up the receiver ready to dial.

"Why don't you just hang here for a while until your mom gets home?" Marc asks. Hamish gives him the evil eye. "Get her some ice, dickwad," Marc shoots back at him. Hamish looks blankly. "In the freezer? Put it in a baggie and wrap a tea towel around it. Use a whole tray of ice. Go."

Hamish goes. Marc shakes his head.

Besides the long thin leather couch and the recliner, the living-room has a glass coffee table and a long red metal storage thingy that looks like a sideways locker on short chrome legs. The TV and the DVD player sit on top of that. I stare at it pretending to find it deeply interesting, but mostly not wanting to look at Marc.

Shawna would freak if she knew I was here.

"We usually hang out downstairs," Marc says. "But I guess it'd be hard with your foot..." He looks toward the hall.

"You have a bigger television down there?" I say, trying to sound teasy, like the Rideau girls at school. He looks down at his knees and blushes, grinning. His smile really is very sweet. I bet he could hold a pen in his dimple if he wanted.

"Let's go," I say, trying to sit up. "I think I can make it." The recliner thuds forward, slamming my foot on the ground. I moan in pain and Marc flashes over to me. Hamish comes running in with the ice.

"Careful, careful. Holy moly. Here," Marc sticks his arm under my legs.

"What are you doing, man?" Hamish asks.

"Taking her downstairs. Get the door."

I'm about to say that I'm too heavy, but Marc lifts me up without so much as a grunt. It seems pretty important to him to get me downstairs. His gray sweater is a little scratchy, but his neck smells like soap.

He carries me to the basement door and I look down the steep stairs.

"Maybe this isn't such a good idea," I say, not sure of how to politely get out of his arms.

"No problem," says Marc. "Hamey, you go first so you can catch her if I fall." Hamish lopes down the stairs still holding the red-checkered tea towel full of ice. I feel Marc take the first step down. He huffs. I turn my head into his chest so I won't have to look.

I feel like I'm a real-live Barbie. I can hear Hamish giggling at the bottom of the stairs.

"You're freaking her out, man," he says, like I can't hear him.

"I'm concentrating," Marc says. Now I can hear the effort. I want this to be over.

And then it is and Marc sits on the couch with me still in his arms so that I'm basically sitting on his lap with my legs over his. I unloop my arm from around his neck and go to slide off him, but he holds my knees with his hand.

"You should keep your foot up," he says. Hamish grunts. I feel myself blush and curl my hair behind my ear. I hope I don't look too sweaty. I hope my armpits don't reek.

Now he knows exactly how heavy I am.

"You really didn't have to do that," I say. My face is

so hot. He's breathing hard and smiling at me with his gorgeous smile. He is so beautiful, I can't believe he's looking at me. I should be allergic to his eyes, but I'm not. I'm looking right at him. It is like looking at the sun.

And he's the one who looks away, down at my foot.

"Hamish," he says. "Ice." Hamish comes over and passes Marc the ice. Marc signals for me to hold up my foot. I lift it into his soft hands and lean back into the corner of the couch, hoping I look casual and not like my left side is all cramped from trying to stay on his lap. He looks me in the eye and presses the ice down on my ankle. I wince and then smile.

I guess he likes me. I feel like an idiot. I can't stop smiling.

Then I vanish from my body and see the three of us in the room as if I were a security camera perched above the stairs. I see Hamish standing there watching us with his television eyes, and me and Marc on the couch like we are lovers in some straight-to-video flick on teen pregnancy.

This is how it starts. The girl falls down, the boy carries her to the couch, the best friend leaves...

"Get us some drinks," Marc hisses at Hamish. I almost laugh. It is like a movie and I am the star. For once.

Hamish disappears back upstairs, leaving me alone with Marc. I zoom back into my body and feel the basement air press against it. I notice the smell of gym socks mixed with spilled Coke and the hum of a freezer against the back wall. The wrinkles of the brown velour couch dig into my butt, which sits heavily on the seat because I don't want my legs to rest too hard on Marc's lap. I feel like my whole brain and heart are mostly in my right leg, because that's where Marc's hands are.

I can feel his hands and there's, like, power coming out of his hands and it's the power of liking me. It makes me breathe harder, but not in a nervous way. It's like how you feel when you wake up after a good sleep and you can feel the warm of the sheets on you and you feel safe even though you know you have a big test at school. You know the nervousness is going to happen, but it's going to happen later and right now, you're just warm. Except for your ankle — I mean, my ankle, which is an aching flesh-ball of throb.

"How long have you known Hamish?" I ask Marc. I hear myself say it. I sound far away.

"Six years. He practically lives here. His dad's a real asshole. He yells and throws these fits over how the newspapers should be stacked. It's better here."

I look around. One half of the basement floor is carpeted, the rest is still cement. I can see they have a skateboard ramp rigged up back there and a basketball hoop. This end of the room is kind of squished toward the stairs with the old brown plaid velour couch and a little paint-splattered wooden stool facing the television. I feel Marc watching me check out the room and can't help looking at him. He's staring at me with his mouth open and his eyes half closed. I quickly look up the stairs.

"I wonder where Hamish is?" I say. The look in Marc's eyes is making me nervous. He pulls my legs more tightly over his lap. "What are you doing?" I giggle.

Dear God. I giggled.

"Shh," he says as he leans in and kisses me.

It lasts a thousand years. I feel the edges of his lips against mine and he cups my head with the back of his hand to hold me up, and he runs his fingers down my neck.

Then it's over. Snap. Like an electric shock.

This is Marc, I think.

Then, I think this. Marc is a fast artist.

His face pulls away and we both look up the stairs. He licks his lips.

"So, you want to go out some time?" His eyes pull at me and a slight heaviness, like spilled Coke air, pushes down on my shoulders.

Hamish is coming.

"Yes," I say quickly, to get it in. Marc pats my foot and readjusts the ice.

Hamish comes down with a tray of drinks and some Cheddar cheese and soda crackers on a plate along with three paper napkins folded into triangles. He puts the tray on the milk crate that's acting as a table and sits down on the wooden stool. Marc fixes me a cheese and cracker as Hamish turns on the PlayStation.

Marc keeps my feet on his lap as he kills pink cartoon elephants with his thumb. Hamish seems to have forgotten that I'm here.

An hour later, Dad calls and I crawl up the stairs and along the hall where I sit by the door to put on my shoes. Marc follows me, laughing as I crawl. Hamish stays downstairs, which is good. Marc opens the door so I can crawl onto the front stoop and then he sits beside me and reaches for my hand.

I can tell he's done this before. I'm happy he has, because I wouldn't know what to do. He brushes his cheek with my hand and I feel his soft skin and I wish he were a blanket I could sink my face into, and thinking that makes me breathe deep.

I can't talk, but it doesn't really seem to be necessary.

He leans over and kisses me again and it's just like drinking water when you're really thirsty. My whole face feels open and all the feeling in my body goes through my lips and into his.

Then I get scared and shift my head to look up the street for our car.

"So, you want to get together tomorrow?" Marc asks.

"Yeah. Um, behind Exit 5?" I say, too fast.

"I'll see you in school. We have science. Want to know a secret?" he asks, which is corny, but cute. I nod. "I wish I got you for my partner instead of Hamish."

"Yeah," I say, like I don't know how to say anything else. Fortunately, Dad pulls up in front of the house then. I pull my hand out of Marc's and he lets me. I go to stand up, but my ankle still kills and I have to hang on to the rail. Marc picks me up again.

"Marc. I'm way too heavy."

"Show off," Dad calls out the window, but opens the door for him anyway.

"I feel like a princess," I say as Marc sits me down in the car.

I can't believe I just said that. What a total knob thing to say. What a girl thing to say. If Shawna ever heard I said that, she'd slaughter me.

I look over at Dad, whose mouth is wide open in this huge grin, and I know that he knows about me and Marc. I get busy doing up my seatbelt.

"See you tomorrow," Marc says.

"Yeah," I say, still fumbling with the seatbelt. And Dad takes off.

"Soooooooooo," he teases me. "He wants you bad, babycakes. Better watch it. Or, actually, I better watch it. Um. Has your mother talked to you about – "

"Dad. Stop it. He just did that because I hurt my foot."

"Yeah, right. He's nice like a snake. A very cute snake, though. And so strong. See how he lifted you into the car like you was as light as a feather. Light as a tiny Thumbelina princess."

I stare out the window at Nelson Street whipping by.

"Gloria's got a boyfriend. Gloria's got a boyfriend," he chants.

There's no use talking to Dad when he gets like this. But by the end of the ride I'm hearing it in my head and it's not a bad tune.

"I probably have a boyfriend. I probably have a boyfriend."

And sometime soon, Shawna's going to know about it, too.

Bad Foot Miracle

After dinner, Mom and Hazel keep me at the table for almost an hour grilling me about Marc.

Mom: "Was his father home?"

Hazel: "Is he into sports?"

Mom: "How long have his parents been divorced?"

Hazel: "What kind of jeans does he wear?"

Mom: "Are they vegetarians?"

"Why does it matter if they're vegetarians?" I ask.

"It doesn't matter. I'm just trying to get a picture of who we're dealing with here."

"We ate cheese."

"Lots of vegetarians eat cheese," Mom says.

"Everyone eats cheese, Mom. That's it. I'm going to call Shawna." I do my best to look as though I'm stomping away, but the bad ankle makes it totally ineffective.

I call Shawna, but her brother Rod must be online because I can't get through. Anyway, I tried. Serves her right if she hears about me and Marc from Hamish. At least now I don't have to ask Hamish to meet me outside Exit 5 after school tomorrow.

Shawna is going to die when she hears. And then she's going to kill me.

I try her number again. Busy. I slam down the phone.

She'll be mad until I tell her about the kissing, which she won't believe. *I* can hardly believe about the kissing.

It happened. I got kissed. I kissed with a boy and it wasn't a game, or a dare, or like we had to because we were relatives at a wedding. It was because he wanted to kiss me, because he looked at my crooked face and wanted to kiss it.

It's almost too much to remember the whole thing. Was it me he kissed? Yes. Did he know what he was doing? Yes. It wasn't a mistake. He asked me to go out with him. He meant to do it.

He likes me. I can tell from his eyes.

Shawna's line is still busy. She's talking to Tina about what she thinks will happen tomorrow. When she's done she'll call me. I won't try again.

Marc kissed me twice. Nobody knows. And nobody knowing is like having a whole tub of Rocky Road ice cream all to myself. Every creamy spoonful of it is mine to enjoy. With my lips. In my mouth.

I try Shawna one last time. She is staying on the phone with Tina knowing that I am trying to call her. This is how she is when she's angry. If only she knew what she was missing. I should have made Dad drive me over there earlier. It's too late now. My foot is killing me.

I crawl upstairs to my room and listen to Hazel tell me stories about her friend Lisa, and how Lisa accidentally stepped on the cat when she was running down the stairs away from her mother during a family fight.

I listen to stories about fighting while I'm kissing Marc in my head. I kiss Marc in my head while I brush my teeth and wash my crooked face. I kiss Marc in my head while I put on my ripped Groovy Girl nightie. I rewind and replay the kisses late into the night, until I can hear my whole family snoring and the wind rustling the dry trees.

•

I still can't walk in the morning so Mom takes me to the doctor to have my ankle checked out and, it turns out, I actually did sprain it. I try not to show how happy I am about getting it wrapped up in this huge ugly peach-colored bandage. When they give me the crutches, I have to pretend that I am truly put out by the whole sore foot thing.

Really, though, I see spraining my ankle as kind of a bad foot miracle. Not only did I not have to walk with Shawna and Tina to school today, I won't have to walk with them for a long time, because it's too far to go on crutches. So there will be lots of time for Shawna to cool off from finding out about me and Marc before I actually have to do stuff with her again. And, if anyone finds out it happened near Marc's house, the crutches are proof that I wasn't faking it to get his attention.

Spraining my foot is practically the best thing that ever happened to me. No one has to know it happened because I was walking down the street with my eyes closed, crying over being manipulated by my best friend who still doesn't know that I've been kissed by the cutest boy in grade nine.

I know it's shallow to be so happy about my foot and beating Shawna to Marc, but I don't care. I want Shawna to see that I'm good enough to get the primo guy. Besides, I do like him and I do want him. It's not like I got him just to get him so that she couldn't have him. That's what she was trying to do to me.

It's not my fault Marc likes me. I like him, too. Not just because he's cute, either. Just because he's good looking, it doesn't make him fake. He's insightful. He knew I wasn't faking it with my ankle. He didn't have to carry me. That was just nice. I think he knows that I'm not all flash and look-at-me, look-at-my-skin, ooh-aren't-I-cute-when-I-pout, that I'm not super cool or prissy like that. I think he can tell I'm just normal in a good way. Like, I wouldn't fake it with my ankle to get a guy. I think he knows that. I'm pretty sure he can tell that.

I have the crutches now, so he'll see that he was right to like me and that I wasn't faking.

"Are you in pain?" Mom asks when we've made it to the car. I shake my head. "Are you all right? Your face is all screwed up."

"I'm thinking about something," I tell her.

"What?" I can feel her looking at me.

"Do you think he likes me? Maybe he was just being nice about my foot?"

Mom's hands drop into her lap and the car keys clink together. I look down at them before looking up at Mom, who has that look in her eye like when I skated for the first time.

"Stop it, Mom."

She brushes my hair back away from my face.

"He'd be crazy not to like you, baby. You're the best thing on legs. Well, on one leg. What's more important is what you think of him."

"I think I like him."

"Do you? You don't have to, you know. You don't have to get a guy just to have a guy. You don't have to do anything you don't want to do."

"Mom. I know that. But what if he likes me?" My stomach flutters as I ask her. I look straight in her eyes.

"Then, that's nice for you." She kisses my head. "Don't you think that's nice for you?" I nod, but I'm not sure. She's about to put the keys in the ignition and then she stops. "I didn't go on a date until I was eighteen, you know. Don't tell your sister. And, just so you know, I got asked out twice before that. If you don't want to go out with him, Gloria, just don't go. Tell him I won't let you, if you want. If you do want to go, then go. All I'm saying is, if it doesn't feel right, it's probably not right. Okay?"

I didn't say I didn't want to go out with him. I didn't say that. I said I liked him.

I want the talk to be over, so I don't say anything and I stare at the car keys.

Mom lets me off in front of the school and gets out to help me up the front stairs.

"I can do it, Mom," I tell her. I poke at her with a crutch to get her to move off. "I'm going to have to do it until my ankle's better. Go."

"Yeah, but this is the first day. You haven't mastered

it yet." She knows I can handle the stairs. She wants to walk me to class so that she can check Marc out.

"You just don't want to go to work," I say. That works. She puts her hands on her hips and frowns at me. She's sick of doing admin work at the courthouse. She says the building's ventilation system feels like it's sucking the air out of her chest.

"I'll see you after school," I say. She shakes her head and gets back in the car.

By the time I get to the science room on the second floor I'm completely covered in sweat from dragging myself up the stairs. I crawled up the last set. I hope nobody saw. I lean against the wall for a few minutes to catch my breath.

Mr. Rokosh is in the middle of a lecture when I walk in. He stops mid-sentence and all heads turn toward me. I'm still breathing pretty hard as I make my way to my seat at the desk beside Hamish. His eyes go wide.

"Broken?" he smirks.

"Sprained," I whisper, leaning my crutches against the desk. I whisper but I know the whole class hears because it's so quiet in here. I look over at Marc and his face goes red. Then Hamish laughs and everyone starts talking.

"Class," commands Mr. Rokosh. "Class. As I was saying…"

I don't hear a single thing that Mr. Rokosh has to say because I'm too busy thinking about the look on Marc's face and trying not to notice Hamish playing with my crutch. Finally, Mr. Rokosh stops talking and the class begins to move around. People are going to the front of the class to get stuff for their experiments. I look at Hamish who has, obviously, been waiting for me to say something.

"Guess I better go up there, eh, winkie?"

"Winkie?"

"Sorry. Do you prefer the term 'cripple'?" He pushes himself out of the desk and goes to the front where he meets up with Marc. I look away out the window. I ate pancakes for breakfast, but my stomach feels empty. My whole body feels empty. I was all excited last night, but now, I don't know, that look on Marc's face. Maybe he's changed his mind. Maybe I was just there and last night was last night and today I'm his best friend's winkie science partner.

I feel Hamish sit back down beside me with the stuff for the experiment. He slides something in front of me. A note. I look at him and he shrugs and fiddles with the bunsen burner.

I open the note. It says: *Lunch? Marc.*

I never thought a boy would ever write me a note. It's like he's reading all the secret wishes in my mind and making every one of them come true.

Hamish is looking at me. I fold the note into my back pocket and take the bunsen burner away from him.

"It goes like this," I show him.

"Yes, mistress," he says and looks over his shoulder toward Marc's part of the room. "So?" he asks, nudging me.

I look over my shoulder at Marc and he's got this waiting look on his face, like he thinks I might say no. Like any girl could ever say no to those dimples. I nod and watch a smile grow on his face.

"It goes like what?" Hamish asks, and I turn back to the desk, where he's taken it all apart again.

"Why did you do that?" I ask him.

"Because I hate you," he says, sending a shiver through me. "Just kidding." He giggles a mean, small giggle and puts the thing back together again.

The whole rest of the class I feel Marc's eyes on my back, but I can't look at him, because I know if I do, my science partner will blow up the school while my head is turned.

•

Marc wants to go to Tasty Burger for lunch. I was happy when he asked me to eat lunch together, but now

I'm not sure. I really have to talk to Shawna. If I don't tell her what happened soon, I might as well lie down in the hallway and let everyone walk all over me because that's what she'll arrange to happen.

In grade five Shawna single-handedly socially obliterated Missy Sanchez by sarcastically imitating her laugh. She did it every time Missy laughed around Evan Trousedale, the boy Shawna had picked out to have her first kiss with. It was kind of cruel and I knew it, but Missy Sanchez's laugh was totally obnoxious and she was showing her new bra to boys at the back of the library on a regular basis — and that's worse than extraneous, that's plain slutty. Shawna never did get Evan to kiss her. Now she claims he was gay. Lucky for Evan he went to West Tech instead of coming here.

"I don't know. Tasty Burger's a couple of blocks away," I say, looking down at my foot.

"You want to go to the caf?" he asks, his beautiful brown eyes sparkling in the fluorescent lights of the second-floor hallway. I can tell he doesn't want to go to the caf.

"Maybe you can just get your food there and we can have a picnic outside," I say. That way I can talk to Shawna quickly and get out of there before she figures out how to punish me for my bad foot miracle.

Marc helps me on the stairs. He puts his arm around

my waist and holds my elbow. As we turn into the caf, though, he takes a few steps in front of me toward the table where he and Hamish and their buddies sit. I hang back looking for Shawna and Tina.

Then I remember that it's Thursday. Shawna doesn't get lunch with me on Thursdays. Tina is here, sitting alone in the corner. She's waving at me to come over. I wave back with my crutch. Marc's sitting down with them at the table, laughing. Why isn't he getting his food?

I don't know what to do.

I hobble over to Tina and stand beside her, watching Marc in my peripheral vision.

"You broke your foot?" she asks me.

"Yeah. No – I just sprained it."

"How?" She pats the chair beside her for me to sit down, but I ignore it.

"I was just walking home and I stepped off the curb the wrong way. I know. It's so stupid."

"Wow, I didn't even know you could do that," says Tina. Then she launches into this story about how she broke her leg when she fell out of a tree at her cousin's farm.

I can see Marc going through the caf lineup. I'm not sure if he'll come get me afterwards or if he'll go back and sit with his buddies. I mean, he agreed to go outside with me, but maybe he's embarrassed by me being on crutches. Maybe he doesn't want his buddies to see him go with me.

"They're an interesting experience, don't you think?" Tina has ended her story and is on to something else.

"What?" I ask, waking up to what she's saying.

"Crutches. They're interesting. They're really helpful, but everyone wants to get rid of them," she says. "My uncle...do you want to hear this?" She looks down at the empty chair beside her. I shuffle sideways so my back is toward the caf lineup. I don't want to see what Marc does. "My uncle eats a lot of donuts. Maybe six a day, sometimes more. He's in real estate and he gets so uptight when he has to meet a new client that he goes to the drive-thru at Tim Horton's on the way. He says it helps him to have something to chew on, and he says the donuts are a crutch. He's so mad about how much he needs the donuts. But, like, you wouldn't take a crutch away from someone with a broken foot."

"Did you tell him to keep eating the donuts?" I ask. Tina looks me in the eye and gives the table a little slap, like I've said something hilarious.

"You don't tell my uncle anything. He says he's going to try to switch to black coffee. One calorie a cup. I never thought I would like black coffee. You have to wait when you first get it or it burns your tongue and – "

"Are you ready?" Marc asks, coming up behind me. Tina's mouth falls open. It is quite satisfying to watch.

"Yeah, I'm starving," I say. "Bye." I give Tina a little half wave and then Marc and I leave the caf together.

Marc holds the door open for me. I have to walk under his arm to go through it, and he puts his arm around my shoulders as I pass under him. I have a weird impulse to shake him off, but I ignore it. I want Tina to see his arm around me even if it does make it nearly impossible to operate my crutches.

It's probably best if Shawna hears about this from Tina anyway. I know they have gym together this afternoon. It's not my fault it's Thursday. Besides, if she hadn't stayed on the phone all night with Tina to punish me, she would have known about it already.

•

It's hard to find a good place to sit outside where it will be easy for me to get up using my crutches. The bad foot miracle is beginning to be a bit of a drag. ("Very punny," Dad would say.) We end up perched on the cement edge of the ventilation shaft facing the teachers' parking lot.

Marc unwraps his cheeseburger and I take my egg salad and tomato sandwich out of the bag. The crinkling of the different packages seems so loud, like it's taking up the whole schoolyard.

It's not really a picnic kind of day. The gray sky presses down on us like wet newspaper. Marc chews his burger and smiles at me and rearranges his fries.

Now he's shy? He's the fast artist. He's the one who kissed me. How can you be shy after you kissed somebody already? I mean, I kissed him, he knows I like him.

"What was it like at Rideau?" I ask, just to say something. He puts down his cheeseburger and dusts the crumbs off his hands over the vent.

"It was all right. They gave way too much homework. I used to get in trouble all the time for not having it done. Don't tell anyone — my mom thinks I might have a learning disability, but Dad won't let me get tested. He says I just need to study more. He's so prejudiced against asking for help. I have to do everything myself. He even makes me darn my socks."

I love Marc's voice. It's kind of low and hummy, and he draws out the words at the end of his sentences, so that they all have three syllables. He flips his hair off his forehead, takes a bite of his cheeseburger, touches my elbow and smiles with his mouth full. Look at his hands.

"Darn socks?" I ask, so I can hear his voice again.

"Yeah, it's like sewing. He doesn't like to spend money on socks. He spends billions on his car, but he won't spend money on socks or paper towels, and he won't buy more than a carton of milk a week because he says me and Hamey drink it all. Of course we drink it all if that's all there is, right? That's why I always order a cheeseburger. I need the dairy."

"Where's your mom?" I say. I like how the skin around his mouth moves when he tries to look serious.

"Toronto. I go to see her at Christmas. Sometimes she comes here when she's on a sales call. She sells these top-of-the-line kitchen counters made of rock – you know, granite. She almost had Dad talked into getting them, but then he got his tax bill. She lives with her boyfriend now. I think she wants to marry him. I could go live with her. But I can't leave Hamey. And if I didn't live here, my dad would sleep on the couch every night."

"It sounds like you're the dad." His hands are big and square and his knuckles look soft. I wonder if we'll hold hands. How do you start holding hands? You can't hold hands with crutches. Are you allowed to hold hands when you're just sitting, or do you have to be walking?

"It is like I'm the dad," Marc nods. I'd almost forgotten what we were talking about. "Sometimes I have to wake him up in the morning because he forgets to reset the alarm Sunday nights. He thinks being a dad is about forcing rules. But he's not there half the time because he's out. He doesn't bring the girls home, though."

Marc looks at me and his eyes dart around my face, like he's remembering who he's with. I swear the skin on the back of my neck feels his eyes on me. He sneaks a peek at my chest. I take a deep breath and swallow the smallest ever bite of egg salad sandwich.

"I can't imagine what it would be like if my parents got divorced," I say. My voice sounds unnaturally high. I clear my throat. "Mom wouldn't let Dad divorce her. She'd lock him in the bathroom."

He's supposed to laugh. Ha. Silence. I press my lips together and pick at the tomato in my sandwich.

Then his face opens to its widest edges and I melt a little inside under the powerful blast of full Marc dimples. He has a perfect little curl behind his ear. It would wrap right around my pinky finger, right around the tip of my nose. Man, he is so, so beautiful. He is the maximum gorgeousness allowable by God. Look at the edges of his eyes. I want to touch his squint wrinkles.

My new future flashes before my eyes. I imagine the two of us with our books open at my kitchen table. I'll sit on his curl side and help him, leaning over, feeling his breath on the back of my neck and stick the eraser end of my pencil in his dimples to see if he can hold it. I will help him with his homework and we'll hold hands under the table. I bet Hazel will try to spy on us. I bet Dad will pay Hazel to spy on us.

My egg salad sandwich drops to my knee. I snap to attention and rub my eyes, getting some sandwich filling in there. I have to use a piece of sleeve to get it out while Marc watches. I am the queen geek.

"You all right, Gloria?"

It's the first time I've heard him say my name, and it makes my heart jump. Then, it's like he felt it, too, because he leans over and gives me a big cheeseburger kiss, holding the back of my head with his hand again. I smell shaving cream smell on his cheek. Warm air blows up through the vent and it's just like a movie, with us kissing and our hair blowing up in the wind of the ventilation shaft across from the teachers' parking lot.

I will never forget this. Ever.

Fall-out

After lunch I have art. We are still working on pen and ink, but now we are supposed to use a wash as well. That's when you add water to the ink. I was going to draw the Martello Tower again because I heard a rumor that Mrs. Bell gives extra points for doing Kingston landmarks, but then I thought I might try to do the outside of the school where Marc and I sat at lunch. You know, for posterity.

I'm a loser artist, however, and the special spot of my movie-star kiss looks like it belongs in a horror flick. I can't get the angles of the walls right. The school looks like it's sinking into the ground.

I get frustrated and pound my hand on the table.

"Here," Tiz says, motioning for me to hand the page over. I push it across the table and sit back with my arms crossed. Let him try.

He gets it perfect in two strokes of his pen. "Put the wash on this side to cover up the other lines." He shoves the piece of paper back and returns to a pair of squirrels he's doing to go with his grandma's rabbits.

"Thanks," I say, watching him draw. He's really talented. Tina told me he was the best artist at Rideau. Which reminds me. "Hey, did you hear about Hamish stepping on a dead squirrel last year?"

"Yes," says Tiz, sighing.

"Why did he do that?"

"You want the real reason?" He sits up and squints at his squirrels.

"Of course."

"I don't know," he says, looking at me as if I'd just picked a fight with him. I don't get it.

"Then why did you ask me if I wanted to know the real reason?"

"I wanted to know if you were interested in the real reason. Why would I know why he stepped on a dead squirrel?" He seems mad. Did I do something wrong?

"I was only asking."

"You're just worried he's going to mess things up for you and your new boyfriend."

Tiz knows about Marc already? Man, word travels fast. I pull my picture closer to me and start applying wash over the lines I got wrong. I feel Tizzy watching me.

He's mad because he likes me.

Why do boys like me now? I don't know how to be the popular girl. That's Shawna's job. I'm supposed to be the quietly excellent easy-going one, the secret best one – like the light under the bushel in the Sunday-school song.

I keep working on my picture and pretend I don't notice Tiz looking at me. The pic looks good once I get going on it, but it's so dark, it looks like nighttime and it doesn't really work to give me the feeling of remembering kissing Marc like I wanted it to. And, anyway, the whole thing's been ruined by Tizzy saying that. I hope he's happy. He sucked the special right out of my movie-kiss memory.

●

After school, I crutch-swing as fast as I can through the halls toward Shawna's locker, my heart pounding from the effort. I turn the corner and there she is. I can't read her face. I pretend to need to look at my crutches as I make my way to her.

"Hi," I say.

"Does it hurt?" she asks. She knows.

"Not really. It just feels heavy. The crutches kill my pits."

"Poor you." She gets busy in her locker, moving quickly for once. She's ticked.

"Mom's picking me up," I say, just to say something, so that she'll say something back so I can tell how ticked she is.

"So?" One-word sarcastic answer equals bad. I swallow for strength.

"I tried to call you last night." I touch her arm and she looks down at my hand and then stares me coolly in the eye. "Don't be mad."

"Why would I be mad?" she lies. "Because my best friend betrayed me. Right." She kicks one of my crutches and I have to balance myself against the lockers. A numbness works over my body and I just barely register Tina making her way up the hall.

"I did not betray you."

"Did you or did you not hook up with Marc and Hamish last night?" Shawna hisses. "Rachel saw you. That's who I had to hear it from. Rachel Pepper."

Uh-oh. That's bad.

"Shawna. It was an accident."

"You are such a liar," she says.

Tina is here now, but I can't look at her, either. My eyes are wet. I bend down to pick up my fallen crutch. I can feel the fury coming off Shawna's perfectly tanned legs.

She slams her locker shut.

"He kissed me," I tell her, and feel the rip in my voice.

I totter, trying to get myself up. When I make it all the way up, I can see Shawna's jaw quivering.

"He kissed you?" Tina asks for Shawna.

"Three times," I tell her. Shawna rolls her eyes. "I didn't mean for this to happen."

"You didn't stop it from happening, either." Shawna puts her hand on her hip.

There's a mini-tornado of anger churning around my sweaty head. I can feel the winds of it ringing in my ears.

"Who could blame her, Shawna?" Tina says. "Would you have stopped it?"

Shawna shakes her head at Tina, but I can sense some give in her. I'm tempted to look at Tina myself, but I don't dare. If Shawna thinks we're ganging up on her she'll lash out like a cornered weasel.

The whole next minute's like a balloon in a pin house.

Then Hamish slouches around the corner, and the clacking of the buckles on his ancient leather jacket breaks the tight silence.

If things had gone according to Shawna's plan, we'd be going to meet him outside Exit 5 right now. But things didn't go according to Shawna's plan and I'm glad. I'm glad how it turned out.

"I gotta go. Mom's waiting." I take advantage and swing down the hall.

"Mom's waiting," I hear her imitate me. "Drama queen."

•

Hazel will not get off the phone. I put the alarm clock on her, but she throws it out the bedroom door when the alarm goes off. Her little friend Lisa is having a crisis about her mom being pregnant by her stepfather. So Hazel's on the phone to her every night while Lisa bawls her eyes out like it's the end of the world. I want to rip the phone out of Hazel's hand and yell, "Get over it," into it.

"You might have to babysit, but maybe you can make them pay you for it," Hazel says. I point at the clock and Hazel turns on her bed so that she doesn't have to see me. She knew it was going to be a long conversation. She even changed into her gray and pink bunny pajamas, like she knew talking to Lisa was going to take all night.

I couldn't talk to Marc after school because of the thing with Shawna and because of Mom coming to pick me up. How are we supposed to set up plans for tomorrow without a phone?

"That's ridiculous, Lisa. They did not wait until you were twelve to get pregnant so that you could legally babysit." Hazel turns enough to roll her eyes at me. "I thought your whole point was that they didn't think about you."

I reset the alarm, then limp down the hall to Dad's office and stand just inside the door until he notices me.

"How's the foot, chickpea?" he asks. He writes guides and reports for the government and spends most of his time typing in sweatpants and a bathrobe, only it's getting cold so he's put a sweater on over his bathrobe and he looks like a demented street-person.

"Can I have a cellphone?" I ask.

"As soon as I finish making payments on the car, get the roof reshingled, buy new windows for the back room, get your mother's tooth fixed and have enough for your first year at university, sure, then I'll get you a cellphone."

"I didn't think so."

"I didn't say no. If you get a job and you want to use your money to buy a cellphone, by all means, go for it. But no can do right now, chickpea. You want a cellphone so that you can be on call for your new boyfriend?" He spins in his work chair and folds his hands together. I adjust my one crutch so it hits my pit in a different spot.

"Hazel won't get off the phone."

"Cellphones are leashes. Don't let anyone tell you

otherwise. They create the illusion of connection, but really — "

"Dad, I didn't seriously expect you to get me a cellphone. Can you just help me get Hazel off so that I can make one short phone call?"

"To Marc?"

"Yes, Dad. That's who I want to call. Why does it have to be such a big deal?"

He sits there looking at me kind of sad and mushy, the way parents go when you don't need their help to reach the cookies anymore. Then he gets up and walks to our room.

"Hey, Haze. Tell Lisa you'll call her back, all right?"

The alarm goes off right on cue and, finally, the phone is mine. I grab it and sit on the bed, letting my crutch fall on the floor. Hazel is still sitting on her bed.

"Do you mind?"

"Fine, forget it." She gets up and stomps toward Dad's office. I bet anything she's asking for a cellphone.

Okay. Now. I'm going to call Marc. I press the first three numbers and then hang up. Maybe I should wait for him to call me? But Hazel will be on the phone again. I dial Marc's number really fast and let it ring. Once, twice. That's it. He's not home.

"Hello?"

"Hi, Marc?"

"Um, I'll get him."

It was Hamish. I cringe. He lets Hamish answer the phone? I hear a video game playing in the background. Hamish says something to Marc. I can't make it out, but Marc says, "Shut up." It's taking too long for him to get to the phone.

Why did I call? The boy should call. It's Friday tomorrow. Boys take girls out on Fridays. If we don't go out, Shawna's going to think it's not real. And it has to be real. He wouldn't have kissed just any girl who came to his house.

I want to hang up. Hazel comes back to the door. I shoo her away and turn on the bed.

"Hello?" he says. I feel like such a girly girl.

"Hi. It's Gloria." As if he didn't know. "I was … wondering if you wanted to get together to do homework tomorrow?" Get together and do homework. On a Friday. What a great come-on. He's just so turned on right now, he can't even talk. Hamish is watching him, too.

"Hey. What's up?" he asks. I don't know what's up.

"I finally wrestled the phone away from my baby sister." From the other room I hear Hazel call, "I am not a baby," and I cover the receiver with my hand. I feel Hamish's eyes on Marc through the phone, and it's like they are on me.

"Why don't you come over? We're just chilling." He breathes deeply into the phone. He does want me. But Mom has the car and she's at her course tonight.

"I wish I could," I say. "But it's too far to walk with my foot and my mom has the car. You could come here if you want."

"Hamish is here," he says, then switches to a whisper. "How about tomorrow? We'll have lunch again and then after school, I'll carry you to my place." He sounds so relaxed, like carrying girls home is what he does every Friday. The hum in his voice tickles my spine, and I try to get the phone even closer to my ear.

"That sounds good," I say, like the whole thing is a new idea. My brain's frozen, but the rest of my body is buzzing.

"Lunch today was nice," he whispers, putting extra *s*'s in "nice." I hear Hamish grunt in the background.

"Yeah, I think I got my dairy, too," I say, trying to be smart, but I can tell Marc doesn't get the joke. "You had a cheeseburger? We kissed?"

"Right," he says. I wait for him to say something else, but of course he can't talk with Hamish standing right there.

"I'll see you tomorrow, Marc." Saying his name is almost like touching him.

"Bye, Gloria."

And hearing him say my name is almost like being touched. I hang up, stare at the phone, then turn around on the bed and both Hazel and Dad are standing in the doorway, grinning like idiots.

"We weren't listening," Dad says. "I was coming to get you off the phone for Hazel."

"You were not."

"You kissed his hamburger? What does that mean?"

"It was a cheeseburger, Dad." I hold the phone out for Hazel.

"She kissed his cheeseburger?" Hazel says.

"I don't understand. Is that code?" Dad asks.

I pick my crutch up from the floor and poke at them with it.

"What do I have to do to get a little privacy?" I try to storm out of the room, but it's hard to stomp with a crutch and a bad foot, and Dad and Hazel won't stop laughing.

•

We're all in front of the TV when the phone rings after ten. Hazel jumps to answer it and then calls for me.

"Probably cheeseburger boy," Dad says to Mom, who's trying to check my eyes.

"And so it begins," she says, reaching for more popcorn.

I take the phone into the kitchen so that they can't watch me talk to Marc.

"Hello?"

"How did that happen with your foot anyway?" Shawna demands. She sounds a little sorry, but I can't be sure, so I just answer the question.

"I stepped off the curb wrong."

"Dough-head move. How long are you supposed to be on the crutches?"

"A couple of weeks. Maybe less. I'm supposed to try putting weight on it every once in a while. I hope it doesn't take too long. My underarms are red from the crutches." Big pause.

"So you guys are really going out now?" She breathes in deeply. Here we go.

"I don't know."

"That sounds like you aren't really sure. You don't know if you're going out with him? You mean he didn't ask you out? Did you ask him out? Because you shouldn't do that. You have to make the guy ask you, otherwise he's not invested. Did he buy you lunch? Rachel said he carried you into his house yesterday. She saw from the store. Is that true? Because that doesn't necessarily mean you two are going out and if, like you said, you don't know, then — "

"I meant I don't know if I should tell you because it's

private. It's between me and him." I let her swallow that. Actually, I'm bursting to tell her all about it. I know I'm going to because — and I knew she would be like this — she doesn't think it's real.

"Lucky ducky you," she says. "Remember how I said you would get a boyfriend first? You didn't believe me."

"Oh, yeah, I forgot." She did say that. And I didn't believe her. Why didn't I believe her? It's like she's apologizing, but her voice is all tight.

"I guess he's your boyfriend. We'll have to see if your relationship with Marc lasts longer than your sprained ankle. Ha, ha. Maybe you can hook me up with Hamish and we could double-date?"

"You want to go out with a squirrel squisher?"

"At least he's got a brain," she says with a fake laugh. "So will I see you at the corner tomorrow?"

"Mom's driving me."

"Oh, duh. Your foot, right? Mm, so I'll see you at lunch?"

"I'm eating with Marc."

"Okay...I'm having Tina stay over tomorrow night. You want to come?"

"I don't know. I'll see."

"It's your foot, Glor. It's not your whole body."

"I mean that I'm supposed to go to Marc's after school and I don't know how late I'll be there. I gotta go, Shawna. Dad needs the Internet. See you tomorrow."

"I guess I'll see you in the hall," she says. She sounds kind of sad, which is the same as her telling me I've won. I hang up.

This is exactly what I thought I wanted to happen. I sit down at the kitchen table under the cat clock with the ticking eyes and lay my head on my arms.

Yummy Yum-Yum

It's raining. The car is warm and I don't want to get out. I have a geography test in four minutes. I lean my head against the fogged-up window.

"I guess you don't have to pick me up after school."

"Why not?" Mom asks.

"I'm going to Marc's," I say, staring at the moving shapes of students out the foggy window.

"This is the first I've heard of it."

"Relax, Mom. We're only going to do homework."

"On a Friday night?" Hazel says.

"What's Marc's last name?"

"Le Clare. He lives on Nelson Street. Dad knows where. Don't worry, we're not having sex." Mom reaches over and puts her hand on my arm.

"Well, as long as you aren't having sex, I guess that's

all right. Remember what we talked about. No cocaine, no heroin."

"I don't think Marc gets enough allowance for that," I tell her. I don't know why I feel so tired today. I got to bed on time.

"Get out of the car now," Hazel says. She has to get to her school so she can run to the washroom and put on lipstick and eye-shadow. I unlatch the door and it falls away from my head.

"Hurry."

I get out and push the door shut with a crutch. Then I have to hustle because the raindrops are those huge pelting kind that feel like tiny snowballs landing on your head.

Tina's waiting for me just inside the front doors. One look in her eyes tells me that she's been sent by Shawna. She knows I know it, too, and smiles a weak smile. She's wearing the wrong pants again. You'd think Shawna would have talked to her about them by now.

"You need help up the stairs?" she asks. She's being too sweet.

I look up the stairs and all the kids marching up them. I don't want to go to class.

"Yeah. Take my knapsack and one crutch." I pull on the handrail and swing myself up. I rest when I get to the landing. "So what does Shawna want?" No sense pretending we both don't know what she's here for.

Tina smiles, this tiny, wee, poor-me smile.

"Why don't you hang out with any of the girls from your old school?" I ask. I don't really mean it to come out as mean as it sounds. I feel my face go red. Tina can't answer. I take my knapsack and crutch back from her and make for geography.

I didn't know I was that angry. The rush of it runs through me all during class, and I'm glad it's a test so that I don't have to talk to anyone.

•

Marc meets me by my locker at lunchtime. I suggest that we go to the Tasty Burger because it's too wet to sit outside and I don't want to sit in the cafeteria with Shawna and Tina watching us. He helps me down to the first floor where Hamish is obviously waiting for him.

Perfect. It's like I'm dating both of them.

I practically punch the sidewalk with the ends of my crutches and take huge hops.

"Don't step on a crack or you'll break your mother's back," I say, for something to say.

Hamish starts walking on the cracks on purpose.

"You hate your mother?" I say to him in the tone of voice he uses with me in science class.

"Quiet. I want to see if it works."

"I'm not doing it," Marc declares. "We need Mom's child support."

The two of them jog ahead of me, each trying to get the other to make a stepping mistake. Then they start running in front of me, trying to get me to shorten my swing so that I'll land in the wrong spot, but I've gotten handy with the crutches and manage to dodge them. We don't talk the whole way there. Turns out you don't have to talk with boys. It's all just pushing and breathing and grunting.

The boys park me at one of the Tasty Burger's window booths and go up to order. I'm sweaty from the work, but the exercise feels good. The smell of the meat pumps through my nose and into my veins. Every time the door opens, another blast of cool air comes in. I slouch down in the booth to try to stay warm.

"But I never told her that."

I'd recognize Shawna's voice anywhere. She's standing right in the doorway, holding the door open. She hasn't seen me.

"She's not stupid," Tina says.

"She's the opposite of stupid. That's why it won't work. Glor's not shallow enough for him. See, now, I'm shallow."

Tina giggles and then she says something I can't

quite make out. I pull my jean jacket over my shoulders. I would shrug down again, but I don't want Shawna to think I'm hiding from her because I'm absolutely not.

"Marc's there, don't look," Shawna says. "Hamish is with him."

"He dumped her already?" Tina says. I quickly look out the window. I can feel Shawna looking for me. Without even looking, I can feel her head turning around. I feel a pin prick on the side of my neck the second she spots me. I can't look.

I'm not going to see her. I don't see her.

The boys shove into the booth. Marc sits beside me. Hamish doesn't even take his jacket off before ripping into his double burger, taking a piece of foil in his first bite.

Marc places my burger, fries and drink in a perfect triangle in front of me.

"I didn't know what you wanted on there, so I got everything except ketchup and mustard. I made her give me packages."

"Thanks," I say. Marc puts his hand on my leg and pats it, making me go stiff in the best way possible.

"You didn't have to ask the lady for the packages. You made her go to the back," Hamish says, speaking with his mouth full.

"It's her job," Marc says.

"She usually puts extra sauce on mine, two swirls, and you distracted her and she only put one swirl. They don't have packages of the sauce."

"Actually, I don't really like ketchup," I say. Marc pats my leg again. "Meat shouldn't be sweet." Hamish kicks Marc under the table.

"Hamey. Stop it. Be a gentleman. Shut your mouth. You've got such bad manners." Hamish straightens up and pulls his shoulders back, then opens his mouth wide to fully display his half-chewed burger.

Marc grabs my knee again and squeezes it. I smile at him and he feeds me a fry, bumping it against my lip to get me to open my mouth. I take it, but I feel a bit ridiculous.

"Hey, your friend is staring at us," Marc says. I know he means Shawna, but I stick to concentrating on my burger. Hamish turns all the way around.

I can't help myself. I look. Shawna's staring at me. I wave and she frowns and juts her chin in our direction.

Hamish turns around. "She looks like she's got a foreign object up her behind," he says in a fake British accent.

I put my hand on Marc's leg and squeeze it. He smiles big and kisses me on the cheek with his mouth still full of cheeseburger.

"So what did you want to work on tonight?" I ask.

He leans over and whispers in my ear, "You."

The word swims through me like the thrill you get when you're next up to fly down the waterslide at Rideau Ferry Fun Park — that exact same fear.

•

This is what it must be like to be famous. All afternoon I catch kids in my class whispering about me, looking at me in the halls and smiling at me like I've done something exciting and bad. The girls from Rideau are especially whispery.

Tizzy wouldn't even look at me in art when I asked about his grandma to try to make things normal between us so that art won't be weird all year. He just shook his head. Rosemary Este lent me her troll-head pencil in math class and when I gave it back to her she said, "You can borrow it any time," and smiled at me like it was such a huge privilege for her to have me use her pencil.

This is how movie stars must feel…and I wish I could tell Shawna about it when I see her waiting for me at my locker after school, leaning against it with her legs crossed at the ankles just above her wedge-heeled sandals. It's too cold for her still to be wearing them, but I know they make her feel tall.

"Hi," she says brightly. I nod and concentrate on getting my lock open. "Listen." Here it comes. "I'm sorry about yesterday, okay? I was just so shocked. I wasn't expecting — "

"What?" I say, letting my lock fall against the metal locker, suddenly furious.

"Gloria," she says, shifting her weight and looking at the wall. Her eyes go all wet, but it's not enough.

"If it was you who got him, you'd expect me to suck it up, to eat it up with two spoons, like yummy yum-yum, how delicious for you. But since it's me…you made it so I couldn't even talk to you about it. Like it was something I did against you. I didn't plan it, you know."

Shawna tilts her head back and shakes her head, trying to swallow the tears with her eyes.

"I said I was sorry."

"You are not." I feel in my veins that I've been waiting for this. Shawna stands there waiting for me to say something else. Why couldn't she let me be happy just one time? Why does every good thing I ever get feel like something I've stolen from her? It's not fair.

"Did you want anything else?" I ask, imitating her sarcasm. She loses it and walks quickly toward the washroom, almost falling off her high heels. I turn back to my lock and do my best to calm down. I finally get it open when Tina comes up.

"Hey," she says. "Have you seen Shawna?" I can tell she's still sore about this morning.

"She's in the washroom. We just had a fight. I'm sorry I let you get in the middle of it this morning. You knew you were in the middle, right?"

Tina doesn't wait for me to finish before she runs off to the washroom.

"Fine. Run away. Go to your master," I say to my locker. "See if I care."

I don't care.

I have a boyfriend now.

Who a Girlfriend Is

I make my way outside to where my boyfriend is waiting for me at the top of the outdoor stairs. Marc's eyes really are so dreamily brown, like Smarties with the color snapped off. My boyfriend puts his arm around me and helps me down the stairs. I let go when we get to the bottom and I start off in the direction of his house, but he takes me by the arm.

"I brought my bike. I'll double-ride you."

He leads me over to the bike rack and Hamish is standing there, waiting for us. Marc unlocks his bike, takes my crutches and hands them to Hamish. Then Marc mounts the bike and motions for me to get on.

"Are you kidding?" I say, trying to smile with my whole mouth so it won't show on my face how freaked I am. Is this me with the bad foot and the boyfriend? Shouldn't I be on my way to Shawna's house to eat lime

Jello and pizza and watch satellite TV while her parents argue about Iraq upstairs?

I'm the one who sets up the cushions in front of the TV. Is that Tina's job now?

"Does her highness need a hand hopping on the bicyclette?" Hamish says in a fake accent, bad French this time.

I get on. Please, God, don't let my wide ass break Marc's bike.

I hold on to the handlebars and close my eyes. I know we are going to crash. It is the price I will pay for choosing a boyfriend over my best friend. This is my job now, as the girlfriend. We will crash and it will hurt, but bring it on. Just let me keep my eyes closed so I don't have to see it coming.

The bike moves off the grass of the school's front lawn and onto the sidewalk. Shaky. Shaky. Now, steadier. Steady. I risk opening my eyes and watch the colored leaves whiz by on the ground.

"You thought we were going to fall," Marc says.

"Yeah," I say. The wind is in my hair. I hold on. The turn's coming up. Here we go. I decide to keep my eyes wide open as the bike bends toward the road. Maybe I want to see it coming. Marc's breath streams past my ear as we bend into the turn. We tip, we turn, we pick up speed.

I always thought my boyfriend would wear glasses, or play the trumpet, or be into canoeing. I never thought I'd have a boyfriend who liked to carry me around. Now I've got a wind-in-my-hair, carry-my-bags, sweet-smile, love-eyes boyfriend and I'm trying to feel him pressing against my back, but it's hard because we're going so fast I can barely catch my breath. And I'm thinking, "This is what it's like. This is it."

We swoop into the driveway and the hill of it slows us down enough that it's not even scary to stop. I climb off, but hold onto the bike for balance.

Marc's eyes are bright and beautiful, like sun shining off creamy chocolate. I want to kiss him, so I do, balancing in the driveway. The two of us are tied together in the middle where we touch. I want to press into him with my whole body to make the feeling be more real. More real even than this cool, wet air pressing on our cold and sweaty tied-together faces and the gulp of fresh breath he steals with his mouth and his hands on my back with the bike between us.

Then Hamish swings in on his bike with my crutches across his handlebars. He's huffing and puffing and stops halfway up the hill of the driveway by the side door. He lets the bike fall beneath him and stumbles up to us with the crutches in one hand.

"I nearly took out this guy's side mirror," he tells

Marc and goes into an elaborate description of turning the corner and the crutches scraping against the side of a car. I go and lean by the side door while Marc puts the bikes in the garage.

He's listening to Hamish, but he keeps looking at me.

•

Marc wants to carry me down to the basement again, but I won't let him. I feel too girly when he does that and I don't want to end up sitting on his lap like before. Not with Hamish here.

I hold on to the handrail, working my way down backwards on my knees. Marc is right behind me carrying my crutches. He passes me on the stairs and waits at the bottom.

"I'm not going to fall, Marc," I say with a smile. He pays no attention and takes my elbow when I reach the bottom step, then weaves his arm around my waist and guides me to the couch.

"Thanks," I say as I sit down. I can hear Hamish drop something upstairs.

"You want a Coke?" he asks.

"Sure." He hands me the TV remote and disappears upstairs. I thought Hamish was getting us drinks. I try to hear what's going on up there, but their voices are

muffled. I turn on the TV and switch around the channels. I know the shows, but it's like I'm watching TV in
a different country — boy country.

I've never really had a lot of contact with boys. I do
know Shawna's brother, Rod, but he's five years older
and into yoga. Before Marc kissed me the other day, the
only other time I got kissed was twice playing kissing
tag in grade five before the yard monitor stopped us,
and another time at day camp when this guy, Ronnie,
pushed me up against the wall outside the dressing
rooms and kissed me on the neck. Or bit me. I'm not
sure. That Ronnie was kind of cute and I guess he could
have been my first boyfriend. He did sit beside me and
try to steal my lunch all the time.

I don't know how to be a girlfriend. I wonder about
Serena, Marc's old girlfriend who moved away, and
what they did together. Tina told Shawna that Serena
was really pretty. Tall and blonde. Figures.

On TV shows and in movies they always show how
the couple gets together and then it's like they go into
some kind of fog and come out of it as either a together couple or as a fighting couple. They never show you
what goes on in the fog. Sometimes they show you a
bunch of scenes with the couple eating ice cream
together or throwing water on each other while they're
washing the car, walking in the park holding hands,

stuff like that. They show you that they are a couple with how they look at each other with dreamy eyes and kissing, but there's always music over top of the shiny new couple scenes and you can't hear what they are saying to each other.

You have to say something when you're with someone in real life. You have to talk. What does a non-fighting girlfriend say?

Maybe I should ask Marc to put some music on.

They're taking a long time up there. I can't hear them anymore. My stomach is nervous. I take a deep breath to try to soften it and flip my hair so that it's pouffy for when Marc comes down. Is a girlfriend supposed to watch TV in the basement until it's time for her to get kissed?

Finally I hear a screen door open and the sound of footsteps. The two of them come barreling down the stairs and Marc flings himself on the couch beside me while Hamish parks on the stool.

"Give me the remote," Hamish says. I pass it to him.

Marc puts his arm around me and I can feel his muscular sides press against me as he tries to catch his breath. Neither of them seems to have remembered that they were supposed to be bringing me a Coke.

"Not 'Millionaire,'" Marc says to Hamish.

"Yes, 'Millionaire,'" Hamish says.

"No. 'The Simpsons,'" Marc orders.

"Ask her," Hamish says.

"I like 'The Simpsons,'" I say. Both of them are focused on the screen now and Marc doesn't say anything. Hamish starts yelling out the answers to the questions before they even put up the multiple choice answers, and Marc tells him to shut up every time he does it. When it goes to commercial, I wait for Marc to argue against the choice of show again. Maybe he didn't hear me.

"Let's just check out 'The Simpsons,'" I say, trying to be tactful. Hamish ignores me and puts the remote down on the floor beside him. Marc seems mesmerized by the commercial on the set. His arm is uncomfortably warm around my neck. I try to subtly readjust. This attracts Hamish's attention and he gives me an evil grin.

"Ask her," he says to Marc.

"Ask me what?" I say. This isn't about choosing a show. Marc shakes his head, still looking at the TV, his mouth open in a half laugh. "What is it?" I try again. Marc looks at Hamish and shakes his head.

"Come on, man. Just ask her," Hamish says, giggling. "Ask her. Ask her." Then he stands up and runs up the stairs. Marc presses his lips together and shakes his head. His eyes go hard. I sit up and look at him.

"Don't listen to him," Marc says, still staring at the

TV. "He's damaged. He's warped in the head." Hamish comes running down the stairs with three Cokes and throws one at Marc.

"You forgot the drinks, a-hole," he says. Marc takes his arm from around me to retrieve the Coke. "Did you ask her?" Hamish asks again. Marc looks at him and the two of them break up. "Come on, man. Please, please ask her," Hamish squeezes out between belly laughs.

What is wrong with him?

"What's going on?" I ask. My voice sounds squeaky.

Marc opens his can of Coke and it fizzes all over the place, setting off Hamish even worse.

"What is with you two?" I ask. Hamish makes a serious face at Marc and this sets Marc off.

Then I get it.

"Are you stoned?" Marc can't stop laughing long enough to answer me.

"That's preposterous," says Hamish. "Whatever gave you that idea? Okay. Marc, snap out of it. Snap out of it and ask her. Come on."

"Why don't you just ask me yourself?" I say. This doesn't feel right. I feel like I'm covered in Coke and like anything I touch will stick to me – like the words that are leaving my mouth are sticking to me like fuzz on gum. They're the ones who are stoned, and I'm the one who feels like she's doing something wrong.

"I'm going to ask her, man," Hamish says.

"Don't. Okay? Seriously, you're being rude, Hame. Just shut up and I'll ask, all right?" Marc turns on the couch so that he's facing me. He looks at me apologetically and then looks over my shoulder at Hamish and loses it a little again. "Seriously, Hame. Don't make that face."

"Just ask it," I say, frustrated. Marc wipes his face with both his hands. His dimples disappear momentarily as he tries to compose himself.

"First, Hamish is not a nice guy, right? Right, Hame?" Marc calls.

"Right," Hamish agrees.

"But he is my best friend. So this is a disrespectful question, but, still, you need to know about it, because it's coming close to you and you should know about it."

"Dun-dah, dun-dah," says Hamish making shark-in-the-water music.

"What?" I ask, sure now that it's something totally stupid.

"Hamish wants to know if your friend…Shawna, right?"

"Right," I say, scared. Marc takes my two hands in his and rubs the backs of them with his thumbs.

"He wants to know if you and Shawna are girlfriends." Marc bursts out laughing at the end. Hamish falls on the floor clutching his stomach. He rolls on the remote, turning off the TV and leaving the room echoing with laughter.

"What?" I ask. "I don't get it."

"Because it looks like Tina and Shawna are girlfriends now," Marc giggles. He still has my hands. I pull them away. Was this why he brought me here? Is this all about Shawna? I feel like I've lost everything. I have to get out of here.

I go to get up, but my foot gives under me and I fall back into the couch.

"Gloria. Glor. I'm sorry. It's Hamish. He made me ask. He's so perverted. Don't leave. It's a joke. It didn't mean anything. He made me. Okay, Hame. I asked her. You can go now. Go."

"But she didn't answer," Hamish says from the floor.

"You said you'd leave if I asked. She's freaked out enough. Just go. I'll call you tomorrow." Marc takes hold of my wrist and I look at him. "Hang on. He's going. I'm really sorry. He made me." Hamish peels himself off the floor, jumps up and sticks his hands in his back pockets.

"You're my science partner," he says to me. "I just wanted to know if you'd done any experimentation." He grins. "Believe me, I don't have anything against girl-on-girl action."

"You are disgusting," I say. The words are out of my mouth before I have a chance to think.

"Hame. Quit it," Marc says. Hamish winks at me and jogs up the stairs. Marc watches him go and listens for the door to close before he lets go of my wrist. "I'm sorry. He's actually not that bad. He's just showing off."

"I don't know," I say, pulling my hair behind my ear. It's so suddenly quiet. I look down into my lap, trying to process what just happened. Marc leans his head so that it comes up under mine and kisses me. His eyes are like fish eyes. I can smell the pot on him now. They didn't ask if I wanted any. I pull away.

He shoves closer to me and puts his arm around me and we stay like that for a while. Then Marc nuzzles into me and I feel myself give and we go all mouths and arms.

I can taste his cold pop mouth and it's juicy, like fresh gum on a winter day. My neck goes weak and I put my hand on his waist to steady myself until we break for air. He looks me in the eye and I feel how much he likes me and how sorry he is about Hamish being a jerk and how relaxed he wants to be with me. We don't need to talk. I take a deep breath and let myself go. I feel his eyelashes brush my cheeks as we make out. The sound of it is wet and gasping.

Upstairs, somebody opens the screen door. Marc breaks off and looks up the stairs.

"That's my dad. You better go to the washroom. He doesn't like me to have girls here." Marc whips off the couch, grabs my crutches and puts them in the bathroom. He picks up the remote on the way back to me and turns on the set. He signals for me to give him my hand and helps me up and to the washroom.

"He's going out tonight," he whispers. "He'll probably go soon. If he finds you, just pretend like you were just coming out of the washroom, all right? Say you're my peer tutor."

He closes the door on me before I can say anything. I sit on the toilet and look at myself in the mirror. My face is all blotchy and red around the mouth. I turn the tap on and let it drip a little into my hands so that I can wipe my face. My heart is slamming against my chest. I try to hear what's going on, but only the sound of the television makes it through the basement bathroom door.

I sit quiet on the toilet and wait for Marc's dad to come down or not come down, to leave the house or not leave the house.

A girlfriend is someone who waits quietly in washrooms, like Barbie in her box.

Monkey Head

The basement washroom is cold and damp. I am all scared and shivery. I don't want to get found. Also, it's almost six o'clock, so there's a chance Mom might call to embarrass me. She always calls Shawna's at dinner time even if I've told her that's where I'm going to be. She says it's her job to check up on me, and that Shawna's the one she doesn't trust, which is such a cop-out. Fat chance she's going to trust me with Marc on a Friday night. And now, if Marc's dad finds me shivering in the washroom and he tells Mom, I can forget about ever getting let over here again.

"Marc's dad, please leave," I mouth to myself in the dark mirror. Is that the phone ringing? The TV is so loud.

I hold my breath so that Marc's dad won't hear me breathe. I hear footsteps on the basement stairs, the television gets muted and Marc's dad asks him if Hamish is here.

"No. He has to go out to his uncle's. It's his uncle's birthday."

"Oh," says Marc's dad. "I didn't know they were close."

"They aren't. Just, you know, his mom…"

"Right. So you're doing your homework?"

"Nothing better to do," Marc lies.

"All right. I'm going to leave money for a pizza in the monkey head. Don't get any pineapple. I hate that crap. Leave me a slice. Don't be a pig like last time. You'll go fat. Also, rake the yard. Today or tomorrow, or some time this weekend. And you will, I repeat, will clean this carpet. I'm tired of my shoes sticking to the floor down here. I'm going with Lena for dinner at the Grill House and then we're going to a movie. Don't look at porn on the Internet or I'll know. You should have more friends than that guy."

"I do, Dad. I just wanted to come home tonight. I think I hurt my ankle."

"What?"

"On my bike. I took a turn too fast today. I think it's twisted."

"Wiggle it for me… Again. Stand up. Walk."

"It's just a little sore. I just didn't want to go out with

the guys because they were going to the arcade and the guy there hates me since Hamey broke the driving wheel…"

"Okay. Good. Maybe put some ice on the ankle and I'll call you later. Understand? No porn."

"Dad. Don't. It was one time."

"Yeah, yeah, sure, sure. You think I wasn't fifteen once?"

Then the TV comes loud again. I'm tempted to look out the door, but am afraid it will be like in the movies and Marc's dad's face will be right there when I open it. So I sit on the toilet and wait.

He was thinking about me when he said that about his ankle.

Marc's fifteen? Did he fail a grade?

Look how red my mouth is. I kissed Marc so hard I think I bruised my face.

Wait. Is that the phone? Is the phone ringing?

Mom is going to know everything as soon as she sees my face. I smile at myself in the mirror to see if I can hide the redness by looking happy.

I hear water running through the pipes. Marc opens the door and it's like I haven't seen in him in days with how my heart goes from one look at his face. He looks worried. That's so sweet.

I feel like there's something wrong with me. Like,

physically wrong. I want him to touch me, but I feel like I'll burst if he does. Or throw up on his jeans.

"You okay?" he asks. "Dad's just taking a quick shower and then he'll go. He's really fast. You want to come out? You might have to go back in when he comes down. Sometimes Hamish just goes under the stairs."

"How fast?" I say, and I get up and hop forward to look under the stairs. He touches my arm to steady me as I go past him, and it feels like getting stabbed in the back — but in a good way.

It's really dark under the stairs and looks kind of squishy. I don't know if I'd be able to get in there without knocking my bad foot around. I might end up screaming in pain. The carpet is sticky, like Marc's dad said, and carpet fuzz gloms on to the tips of my crutches.

I listen for the shower. Is that the phone?

"I should go, Marc. While he's still in the shower," I say. Marc's face falls. I want to touch it. I want him to come close. Maybe it would be all right…

"He'll only be a minute. Don't you want to stay for pizza?"

Something falls in the bathtub upstairs and we both look up and hold our breath, but the shower sound continues. He's just as scared as I am. I don't want to get caught.

We haven't even talked yet. We shouldn't be making out, no matter how much I want to swallow his eyeballs or lick his chin.

God. I really have to go.

"I better go. My parents will call here if I'm not home for supper."

"But you said it's too far to walk."

"I'll be okay. They might even call while your dad's still here so you better answer the phone if it rings. I should go. I had a good time," I say. "Really, really good." I hear myself sound a little too enthusiastic. Then we kiss again. I feel like I'm melting in fast motion. And then I see our reflection in the TV screen. He looks amazing and delicious and I look smushed and awful.

I've got to go. Now. I break it off and crawl quickly up the stairs. The sound of water in the pipes stops as I hit the kitchen. I notice a ceramic monkey head on the windowsill. I hustle to the back door and he holds open the screen door for me.

"I wish you didn't go," he says and leans down to kiss me goodbye.

I'm so good at kissing, I can't believe I never did it before today.

"Bye," I say, and he lets the screen door shut and stands there as I make my way down the driveway.

I put some steam into it as I cut through Victoria Park. I have to get home to call Shawna. Maybe it's not too late to make up and stay the night over there with her and Tina.

What's the use of having a boyfriend if you don't have someone to tell about it?

I stab the ground with my crutches, crunching and killing fall leaves beneath them. I toss my head back as I swing through. Forward, swing, forward.

"Ee-ee-ee-ee!" I'm swinging like a monkey – a wild woman monkey, crazy in love and free as the wind whipping through my mussed-up hair.

•

Mom has the phone book open on the dining-room table when I get in the door.

"I was just looking for Marc's number," she says.

"It's not even seven o'clock, Mom," I argue, relieved I got home before she had a chance to talk to Marc's dad. "Don't go hyper just because I have a boyfriend now."

She flips the book shut.

"I am going to be hyper about it and you're just going to have to put up with it. So?" She follows me into the kitchen where I hobble over to get a paper towel to wipe the sweat off my face. Hazel is sitting at the table reading a magazine.

"So, what?" I say.

"Give her something, Glor," Hazel says. "She's going mental. She wouldn't even let me call Lisa in case you were calling from Marc's."

"No, Hazel. You can't call Lisa because Lisa's grounded and, as I just found out, she's not allowed to use the phone." Mom's talking to Hazel, but the information is meant for me. Hazel rolls her green eyes at me to let me know just how deeply hyper Mom's been.

"All right," I say, and Hazel closes her magazine and pulls her chair tighter to the table. Mom sits the edge of her butt on the counter. I have their complete attention.

"Don't worry, Mom. Hamish was there, too. We went to the basement and watched 'Who Wants to Be a Millionaire' and drank Cokes. They were going to order pizza and that's when I said I had to come home because you were probably freaking out. Exciting enough for you?"

"Who is this Hamish?" Mom asks.

"He's the one, I told you, who stepped on the squirrel. He's Marc's best friend, which I'm not crazy about. He asked if Shawna and Tina were girlfriends, like lesbians, and he was so mean about it."

"Maybe he's in love with Marc and that's why he wouldn't leave you two alone," Mom says. Hazel's jaw drops.

"Mom," I moan. "It's not a soap opera, it's real life."

"Stuff like that happens in real life, too, Gloria. It's a perfectly reasonable working hypothesis. Homophobia can be a sign of homosexual interest. I'm not saying he's gay, but it's not unusual for boys his age to – "

"You're as bad as he is, Mom."

"All right, forget it. All I'm saying is I'm thinking I might go back to university to get my psychology degree. What do you girls think of that?"

Me and Hazel look at each other and we're both thinking the same thing.

"Aren't you a bit mature for university?" Hazel says. "And by mature, I mean old." Mom crosses her arms and looks at me.

"I wonder at the expense," I say, which is what she has said to me about horse camp and sailing camp and non-day-of-the-week new underwear. "Dad's already making some pretty interesting sandwiches."

"You mean gourmet sandwiches," says Dad, walking into the kitchen with his chest puffed out through his sweater over his bathrobe.

"It's not gourmet if you use ketchup because we ran out of mayonnaise. It has to be what you meant it to be for it to be gourmet," I argue. "I couldn't eat it, by the way. Marc had to treat me at the Tasty Burger."

Then my whole family goes, "Oooooooooooo," and I

blush so hard my face goes red like it's been fresh hard-kissed.

"Isn't that special?" Dad says, giving me his googly eyes like he knows exactly what went on in Marc's basement after Hamish left, like he was there, listening at the top of the stairs.

I can't help it. I look down at my lap, grinning like an idiot.

•

Then we get in this big discussion about Mom maybe going back to university to become a psychologist. It turns out Nana said that she would be willing to lend Mom some money toward it and might sell the old house in Vancouver and buy a condo here now that she's retiring from teaching. Mom and Nana don't usually get along, so the deal sounds like it might be good or it might be bad. We agree that if it means that Nana's heart has changed about Dad and us and that she's trying to make it up to Mom in a sincere way, then it's good. If it's Nana not knowing what to do with herself and deciding to spend her free time trying to manipulate Mom, then it's a bad thing. Mom thinks that it doesn't matter what kind of thing it is if she can get a higher education out of it. Dad agrees and will try to be nice to Nana, but admits he will probably fail.

Me and Hazel will get the most out of Nana moving here because it's not our fault we were born children of an imperfect union and we will get spoiled with Nana's teacher pension money. But Dad says Hazel has to wait until she's fifteen to ask Nana for a cellphone. I won't ask Nana for anything because that would be greedy.

I'll just see what she feels like giving me.

I wonder if Marc's mother will like me?

"Crap," Mom says. "How'd it get to be so late?"

I look up at the moving cat's-eyes clock and feel panicky. It's almost too late to call Shawna. Hazel takes one look at my face and dives for the phone. I'm handicapped by foot, but still run after her.

"I just need five minutes. I swear to God. Please, please. Hazel," I yell up the stairs. But I can already hear her pressing the buttons.

"Mom, she's calling Lisa."

"Get her off the phone then. I'm tired of refereeing phone usage between you two. Figure it out."

I can tell she's going to be acting all psychology on us all the time now. Great.

Shawna and Tina are probably in their pajamas already. What could I say anyway that wouldn't sound like I was just making up with her so that I could brag about Marc? I sit on the stairs and think about it. But, since the only real reason that I want to call Shawna is

116

to make up with her so that I can brag about Marc, I can't think of anything to say that isn't going to sound like what it really is.

It's not my fault that Marc likes me. She has to get over that. She knows it, too.

Mom calls for me to set the table. I go into the dining-room and sit down.

"Me and Shawna had a fight," I tell her. "She's jealous because of Marc." Mom nods and winds her hand in the air for me to go on.

"And?"

"And, we don't have many classes together because I picked art and she picked drama, right? So she's got this new friend, Tina."

"The one with the bad pants who Hamish thinks is Shawna's girlfriend." Mom remembers everything.

"Yeah."

"So Shawna's jealous of Marc and you're jealous of Tina," she says. I sit there trying to feel if I'm jealous of Tina.

"I'm not jealous," I say slowly.

"Of course you aren't. You're the one with the boyfriend." Mom gives me a sly smile.

"Shut up."

"Hey," she warns, holding up her finger. "Don't shoot the messenger. You do like Marc, don't you?"

"He's the cutest boy in school, Mom," I inform her. She makes her way to the kitchen where Dad is cutting extra onions into canned tomato sauce for a quickie pasta dinner.

"Notice you didn't exactly answer my question," Mom calls back. "Forget setting the table. It's late. We'll eat in front of the TV."

I sit in the dining-room until dinner's ready, listening to Hazel be on the phone with Lisa when she's not supposed to be, and to my parents moving around the kitchen totally in sync with one another.

My parents are like nothing I've seen in any movie. I catch phrases like "The one with the yellow crack in the thingy," and "another elephant hair's worth," and "a case of bad pants envy," and "you cut my damn toenails if they gross you out more than curdled milk in coffee."

Dad falls asleep in his chair in front of the TV, and we put wet spaghetti noodles on his forehead before turning off the living-room lights to go to bed.

Boyfriend Country

When I get up, I unbandage my foot and try to walk on it. It's still pretty sore. I was thinking that I might as well just go over to Shawna's this morning. It would be too hard talking with her on the phone knowing that Tina's right there listening while Shawna makes faces at her the way she always used to make faces at me when she was on the phone with Rachel Pepper. At least if I'm there in person she'll have to be careful with her face.

My foot hurts. Does it really hurt, or am I just afraid to go to Shawna's?

It hurts.

I wish I had someone else who I could talk to about kissing Marc. Someone who wouldn't feel jealous, wouldn't tell my parents and wouldn't blab it all over school.

Wait. There is someone.

Marc picks up on the second ring. Now that I have him on the phone, I'm not sure what to say.

"Hey," I say.

"Hey. What's up?"

"I just wanted to talk to you." Now I feel really stupid and start fiddling with my foot bandage, winding it around the chair. I don't know what to say. I cover the receiver end of the phone and let out a deep breath.

"That was nice last night," he says. "On the couch. You've got a really great mouth." It sounds like he's cupping the receiver with his hand. I feel my neck go hot and take a fast suck of air.

"But my smile's all crooked," I say softly.

"I know," he says. "It's so hot. We should meet. You want to meet?"

"Now?" I ask hopefully.

"I have to go shopping with Dad. Later. Maybe we can go to a movie? I'll come get you around five."

"You know where I live?"

"Yeah. I looked your address up in the phone book to see how far you had to go. That's kind of far on crutches. You should have waited."

He looked me up in the phone book. That's so sweet.

"If my dad found out that we were alone together in your basement, he would have killed you first and asked questions later," I say.

"Oh," he says. "That's not good. I guess I have to watch my step. Just like you — with the crutches."

"That's me. Injury Girl." This makes him laugh. I twist the bandage around my waist and tie myself to the chair.

I made him laugh. Introducing Injury Girl. Comes complete with crutches and bandage, can make boyfriend laugh, might have nice hair.

As soon as I get off the phone I get busy putting foam on the tops of my crutches so they won't dig into my pits so much. Now I can go over to Shawna's. It's time to T.C.B.

Take Care of Business.

•

I pick up a bag of red licorice on my way. It's a peace offering, so when Shawna opens the door with that sarcastic look on her face I have something to shove at her.

"Here," I say, practically throwing the licorice at her before I have a chance to get nervous and lose my Injury Girl edge. "Can I come in?"

"Why?" she says, and stands in the doorway, still wearing her blue flannel PJs with the dog-bone print and with her hair stuck in a falling-down bun on top of her tiny doll head.

"Because, you know why." She still won't let me

through. We've never fought like this, where it's been more than a day and we both know it's a fight. Usually Shawna doesn't know I'm secretly fighting with her. Except for the last couple of days, our most major arguments have mostly taken place in my head on the way home from school.

I try to look around her.

"Is Tina here?"

Shawna leaves the door open and turns down the hall. I hobble through and close it behind me. When I get to the breakfast nook, Tina's sitting there in front of a grilled cheese sandwich and ketchup. Her hair's all greasy and stuck behind her ears, and she's wearing an oversized black T-shirt with a picture of a cartoon angel on it. Shawna sits in the booth and crosses her legs.

"What did you want to say?" she says.

"I don't want to fight anymore."

"I don't hear any fighting? Tina, do you hear any fighting?" Shawna's not going to make it easy.

"Tina, I like you," I say. Tina perks up and wipes the crumbs off her mouth with the back of her hand. "I guess… I was a bit jealous of you and Shawna. It seems like you two are always together and I feel kind of left out."

The last sentence is squeezed out of a tight throat.

When I practiced the speech in my head on the way

over, I thought it would be a way of making Shawna feel like she had something over me, so that we could be even. She could be jealous of Marc and I could be jealous of Tina — just like Mom said. I didn't think I actually was jealous of Tina. But now it feels in my throat like I am, and I have to hang on to the kitchen counter to keep my balance.

"It's not like we were deliberately excluding you," Shawna says, and Tina nods.

"I didn't think that," I say, even though I did think that. "It's just, we don't have classes together anymore and I knew you'd make new friends, but I didn't think you'd get so tight with a new girlfriend — "

"You mean tight like you and Marc?" Tina interrupts.

"Yes. I guess you're right. It's like me and Marc. I didn't think it would be so fast with everything. Like, before you know it, you're making out." I take a deep breath.

Shawna uncrosses her legs, sits up at the table and opens the bag of licorice.

"You guys made out?" she asks, looking up at me.

And, just like that, fight's over. I tell them about double-riding on the bike and kissing in the driveway. I tell them about those guys getting stoned and not asking me to join them. Shawna says Marc probably was afraid I'd leave if he asked me, which, coming from her is kind of a compliment. Tina says that Hamish was supposedly stoned when he stepped on the squirrel, but that it wasn't certain or she would have told us about it already. Then I told them about the basement, which I wasn't going to tell them. I leave out the part about Hamish making Marc ask me about girl-on-girl action, because I want to tell about the kissing and I don't want them distracted. Then I tell about the kissing and they both listen with these great looks on their faces. Then Shawna asks me if Marc touched my boob.

"No. That's not why he likes me," I say.

"I never said it was, Glor."

"Bet he tries," Tina says.

That isn't why he likes me. He said my smile was hot. Lots of girls have big boobs.

"Kissing is so great," I say, to get us back on track.

Then we each talk about every kiss we've ever had. I say about how I wish I'd kissed Ronnie from camp. Then Shawna tells her Lawrence skinny-dipping story in long, excruciating detail, focused heavily on his "thing."

Then it's Tina's turn.

"We were in the garage behind the old freezer and we were playing Sardines. You know Sardines, where the It hides and then you hide with the It when you find them? I was It and I didn't think anyone was going to find me and then, next thing you know, we're kissing. But then we both heard my cousin outside. He was crying because he couldn't find us and so we stopped kissing."

"Why was he crying?" Shawna says.

"We used to be so mean to him," Tina laughs. "We made him take a taste test once and we put hot sauce on one of the crackers. He screamed so loud. We were only eleven."

I can tell Tina's embarrassed not to be able to offer up a more recent experience. Like me, before this week.

"Who was it you kissed?" Shawna asks. Tina looks at me as she answers.

"This neighborhood kid."

"Do we know him?" Shawna asks.

"No. Moved out west." Tina picks up grilled cheese crumbs with the end of her finger and licks them off. She shoots me a weird look – a look like a dare, like I might try to cut her away from Shawna. But she's not allowed to be jealous of me and Shawna because we've been friends forever and she's the one who's new.

"Marc says I have a hot mouth," I tell Shawna. The impressed look on her face is the whole reason I had to make up with her today.

"You do," says Tina. "Your lower lip kind of goes to

the side when you smile. It makes you look like a cow-girl."

"A cowgirl?" Shawna laughs.

"Yeah. I saw a picture of one once in a magazine. It was about a rodeo and she was swinging a rope around her head."

I kind of get why Shawna likes Tina. That girl has the strangest mind.

"Who does Shawna look like?" I ask her. Tina looks at Shawna and smiles.

"She's a tiny dancer, like in that Elton John song. My mom has it on this mixed tape my dad gave her in college. 'Hold me closer tiny dancer.'"

She sings with so much energy that we have no choice but to join in. Never mind we don't know the words.

•

I made Dad come pick me up at Shawna's at four just in case Marc got here early and now it's 5:13 and Marc's still not here.

I'm sitting in the kitchen looking at the cat's-eyes clock while Mom and Dad sit out on the back deck drinking wine and flipping through the Queen's University course calendar. It's too late for Mom to start this year, but she's hoping she can still get in to one of the correspondence courses so she can at least start working on getting some credits.

Dad looks back into the kitchen.

"Stop looking at me," I say. He puts on his warning face and says something to Mom. "Maybe he's lost, Dad," I say. Then Mom looks at me. "Stop looking!"

Mom's eyes go to the clock. I wish I had a blanket I could throw over it. I cross my arms on the table and plunge my head into them.

This day was going too good. I should have known that it would crud up. I've had too much lucky princessness lately, with the bad foot miracle and the getting my best friend back and the finding out I have a cowgirl mouth. It's too much good. So God has to balance it with making my boyfriend forget about our date.

I press my eyes into the flesh of my arms and try to black out the world by concentrating on bouncing my breath off the table. I brushed my teeth three times and can feel the mint breath tingle in my nose.

I tune into a hum coming from outside somewhere. Not a hum. Skateboard wheels. I peel my face off my arms, hop quickly to the front door and throw it open.

"He's here," I call back, but I don't think they heard me. "I'm going now."

I grab one crutch and stumble out the door. Marc is

flipping on his skateboard in his long shorts. His brown knees are scuffed and his arms hang in the air reaching for balance. He flips the board, lands the jump and arcs around on the road, landing in front of my house with a killer smile on his face.

"Hi," I say and feel so suddenly aware of the edges of my cowgirl smile that I have to look away.

He leans forward and kisses me, keeping his Smartie eyes open, which I only know because I didn't have time to close my eyes. I'm never closing my eyes again.

"You're late, young man," comes Dad's voice behind us. He and Mom are standing in the driveway. They saw us.

"Hey," Marc says, putting his hand out. Dad seems to approve of the handshake. Mom's hanging back a bit, smiling at me with her I'll-get-you-later teeth. Marc nods at Mom, who salutes.

"That's a mighty sporty board you got there," Dad says. "What'd that run you? A hundred and fifty, something like that?"

"My mother bought it for me." I like the way he says "mother," like he's trying to be extra polite. Mom catches it and walks up to where Dad's standing.

"You guys can go," I tell them. Dad winks at me and crosses his arms. Then Mom crosses her arms. Then I hear the front door creak open and Hazel's coming out

128

and she's wearing her red shorts, which are way too short for her now.

"You guys are killing me," I say under my breath. Dad puts his arm around me.

"So, Marc. You should be a little scared of me. All right?" Dad says. I am dying. I am so deeply dying. "And her," Dad points at Mom. "I'm basically a good guy, but Gloria's mother has very long nails and looks for opportunities to use them. She enjoys inflicting damage, and she can't wait for the day our oldest, dearest, darling daughter's boyfriend is the least bit disrespectful. Ain't that right, honey?"

"That's right," Mom says.

"Come on," I protest, stomping my crutch.

"Why'd you call Gloria the dearest daughter?" Hazel demands from the porch. Mom turns around and waves her hand at Hazel to go back in the house.

I am mortified. Dad pulls me in closer to him. I can smell his winey breath and his pits. I look down and try to stand very, very still.

Oh, my God, Dad's fly is undone and his paunch is poking out a rip in his T-shirt. I close my eyes and pray for it to be over.

"Okay," says Marc, and then, "sir."

"You've got really lovely eyes," Mom says.

"Mom," I mutter.

"Why is Gloria the dearest?" Hazel demands, walking up beside Mom. I muster my strength and break out of Dad's grip.

"We're going now. Let's go," I tell Marc.

"Good day," Marc says.

"Be home before ten or I call the cops," Dad calls. "Nice meeting you, Marc."

I move as fast as I can down to the corner. Marc skateboards on the road beside me doing circles because I'm so slow. I don't feel like I can talk to him until my family is out of sight.

As soon as we're on Frontenac Street, I stop and lean on a tree. Marc skateboards up to the next driveway and then circles up onto the sidewalk and back to me. His jaw is loose and his eyes look sore.

"That was completely horrible. I cannot believe them. If I had known they would do that, I would have met you at the park or something." Marc picks at a tree and stares off into the sky above the park. I feel bad for him. I touch him on his elbow. "I didn't know. I never…a boy's never come to pick me up before." I turn my head toward the tree. I can't look at him. I can only look at his chest. His green jersey looks brand new.

He dressed up for me. My heart sinks into the roots of this big old tree. I lean my head against it.

"At least they let you out," he says, and I can hear in

his voice how scared Dad made him. He clears his throat. "Did I do something wrong?" He sounds so far away, it pulls me to him and I touch his side with my free hand. I do it without thinking. I'm not scared.

"No. They're just like that. My dad thinks he's funny."

"He sounded serious."

"So did you. 'My mother gave it to me,'" I imitate him, trying to tease him out of it. He does smile a little. "And 'good day.' What was that? You sounded like Mr. Rokosh." He smiles wide enough to activate the dimples and tucks his skateboard under his arm, taking my non-crutch hand in his.

"Does Mr. Rokosh say that?"

"Every day at the end of science," I say. His hand is so smooth and he rubs his thumb over my knuckles. He's a good hand-holder. So expert at it that thinking about his hand makes my mind go blank.

"I don't know. Maybe I did get that from him. I just said it. What else did I say? All I remember is your mom's fingernails. Why'd your dad say they were long? They weren't long. They were totally normal. My mom has long nails. She gets them done."

I love his voice in my ear. I want him to keep talking forever.

"I know. I don't know why he said that about Mom's

nails. She bites her pinky nail when she watches TV. Not all of them, just her pinky. Freaky deaky."

"Freaky deaky," he repeats and squeezes my hand. Then I feel him being beside me, like a radiator, radiating that power of Like. It's pouring over the side of me that doesn't have a crutch and it's making me swallow and making the spot where my neck meets my shoulder tickle and ache at the same time. I try to brush the spot with my chin and Marc catches me and lets go of my hand and brushes my hair off the spot for me.

He is electric and I am water.

He takes my hand again and we make it to the park and onto a park bench. He is telling me about his mother, but I can barely hear him because I am busy watching his hand play with my hand.

"Mom was supposed to come in a couple of weeks, but she might not come because her boyfriend doesn't like it when she and my dad meet. Her boyfriend likes it when I go there. He doesn't like me, but he thinks it's better if I go there than if she comes here. He's a banker." Marc says banker like it's a dirty word and looks at me like it's supposed to explain everything about his mom's boyfriend. So I nod. Banker equals bad. Got it.

He goes on. "The guy doesn't trust her. But if she's coming through town anyway – she's not exactly coming through town, but Kingston is on the way to Ottawa where her meeting is. It's almost exactly halfway and she has to stop for gas or lunch sometime…"

"And to see you," I say. Our hands are still together. His nails are short and clean and white against his goldy skin. This is what boys' hands must be like. Big. Square. Warm.

"Yeah. She has to stop anyway. Dad could drive me up to the Pizza Hut or I could take the bus. I should tell her that."

"Or she could come down to see you," I say, folding my fingers between his fingers, feeling his fingers between my fingers, making a finger sandwich of fingers. "We don't have to go to a movie if you don't want." Salty finger sandwich. I'm a little hungry. But also, I'm thinking that Shawna might show up at the movie theater since I made the mistake of telling her and Tina that me and Marc were going there tonight. I wouldn't put it past her to "accidentally" run into us on our first date.

Where could we go where she wouldn't go?

"My mom won't come down, though. She might, if I asked her. But if Dad asks her, she won't."

"Why don't we go to McDonald's? Or we could go to Morrison's." Morrison's has good booths and cheap food. It's a bit of a walk, but not if we have all night, and it beats popcorn for dinner and Shawna watching us.

"I could ask her. I got two weeks. I could save for a taxi to the Pizza Hut."

"My dad will drive you if yours won't."

"It's not like that. He would drive me, but if he knows she's coming…then he wants to see her, and then he'll ask her to come and then she won't come. Your dad would really drive me?"

"Or just ask to meet her downtown." On second thought, I don't like the idea of him spending more time with Dad.

He shakes his head and goes quiet. I am concentrating on the halfmoons of his thumbnails and thinking how they look like burger buns and, then, of how Marc bought me lunch at the Tasty Burger the other day. He is so sweet. I squeeze his hand.

"Of course she'll come see you. She loves you. You're her son," I say, leaning my head on his shoulder.

Marc pushes me off and looks at me like I just hit him.

"Are you all right?" I ask.

Marc lets go of my hand and turns on the bench so that I can't see his face.

"Marc?" I don't know what to do. I put my hands in my lap and look out across the park. My hand is suddenly cold. I feel like I've just landed in the park, and it's like I'm in a park in a different country.

I am in Boyfriend Country, and I don't know the customs or the language. The feeling seems to stretch to the houses on either side of the park and all the way down to the lake.

It is like being in Stanley Park in Vancouver when Nana went to get the car and didn't come back for forty minutes and I didn't know her phone number. What was I supposed to do?

Thinking about Stanley Park makes me wonder about Marc's ex-girlfriend, Serena, who moved out west. Did she know how to be a girlfriend? Am I like her? Is that why Marc likes me? Does he miss her?

I think that maybe Marc is crying, but I can't figure out why and don't want to ask, because it might be the wrong thing to do. So I just look out and wait. Eventually I focus on a guy sitting against the door of the park's utility building.

Hamish.

Why am I surprised?

"Why don't we go down to Morrison's?" I say again. Marc puts his arm around me, pulls me into him and kisses my head. I guess I didn't say anything wrong.

He stands up, helps me to my feet and takes my hand as we start down the path out of the park toward downtown. When we get to the edge of the park, he kisses my hand and looks at me shyly.

"Should I call him?" he asks, pointing to Hamish with his thumb.

"Did you know he was there?"

Marc shrugs. Maybe he's having trouble being in a new country, too.

"Your choice," I say. He looks toward Hamish, trying to make up his mind. "Go on," I say, because I can tell he wants his buddy with him. Marc whistles and Hamish gets up and takes his time walking toward us, yanking at his big-ass pants to keep them from falling down. The sun's behind him, so I can't see his face and I don't want to.

I let go of Marc's hand to readjust my crutch.

"Maybe I do feel like going to a movie," I say.

If Hamish is going to be there, then who cares if Shawna and Tina show up? I hope they're there. I want Shawna to see me hold hands with Marc.

•

Hamish wants us to see a restricted horror movie, but they ask Marc for ID when he gets to the ticket booth. He and Hamish break out laughing and we have to go to the back of the line again while we figure out what "PG piece of twitty-assed crap" (Hamish's words) we're going to see. I only have enough money for a fourteen-or-under ticket and a small bag of popcorn, so I don't mind. I don't like horror movies anyway. They give me nightmares about getting shot and still having to run forever even though I'm shot and I don't know which way to run.

I don't know why people pay money to see stuff like that. I'd pay to have it extracted from my head.

Marc hasn't let go of my hand the whole night. Every time Hamish says something that's supposed to be funny, Marc looks at me and laughs like he's sharing the joke with me, like he wants me especially to get it, and I can't help smiling back at him because he wants me to so badly.

But mostly I wish I had some kind of textbook to get me through the night in Boyfriend Country. I keep looking for Shawna and she keeps not being there.

When we get in the theater, Marc chooses seats on the far side of the second-last row and makes Hamish sit a couple of seats away from us. We didn't even get popcorn and my stomach is growling a bit. Marc paid for Hamish, so he probably didn't have enough money for popcorn. It wouldn't be fair for me to have some and them not to. If I had enough cash for a large, then maybe I would have got some. I hope Marc can't hear my stomach.

The lights go down and he puts his arm around me so that his palm fits to the shape of my shoulder exactly.

I brush the back of my neck against his arm. So soft.

The movie is a teen comedy, but the jokes are super lame. Like, the heroine accidentally dyes her hair green. Lame. Man slips on dog poop. Lame.

Five minutes after the credits, Hamish gets up and loudly leaves the theater. As soon as he is out the door, Marc moves his hand — I can see it coming toward me in my peripheral vision — and he strokes the side of my neck. I can hear him breathing. It is not movie-watching breathing. He rubs my neck and I let my head flop onto his shoulder.

In the dark I can only make out the underside of his chin and his Adam's apple. He swallows. I see it. His head turns and his nose comes toward me, silhouetted against the big screen. His face closes in on mine and I keep my eyes open to watch his eyelashes move like the legs of baby spiders. I am so glad I brushed my teeth.

He brushes his dry lips against my cheek searching for my mouth. I let him find it on his own so that I can notice the way his face works from close up. I am hot soup and he is cooling me down with his breath until… he finds me and I no longer have a head. I close my eyes and dive into the sensation of our mouths working on one another like juicy skin suction cups.

It is how I remember it from yesterday. It is good. Primo.

I reach my hand for his neck to hold him there and he tightens his arm around me, moving his hand under my arm and onto my breast.

I break it.

"Sorry," I whisper. That was…too good. We are both breathing heavily. I look down the row and see that Hamish has not come back. Marc takes my hand and we play with our fingers and pretend to watch the movie. A car-chase scene. A stink bomb. Underwear falling from the sky.

Marc's mouth. Here we go again. We go and go, and he doesn't try to touch my breast again, which is good, because I might have let him — and then what?

I love kissing. I don't know why people aren't kissing everywhere all the time, every single minute of every single day.

Then he breaks it off and smiles at me in the dark.

"I'm going to get a drink," he says.

"Okay," I whisper. He lets go of my hand but doesn't move. I try to turn my attention back to the movie, but I'm totally lost. Something about a teacher? No. A bad psychiatrist. My face is a little sore and the skin around my mouth is throbbing. I press my hands to my mouth and giggle, trying to catch Marc's eye. Then he gets up and makes his way out the door. I clench my fists in excitement and take a few deep breaths.

I'm really doing it. I'm really having a boyfriend.

"So, pretty hot stuff," comes Hamish's voice behind me. I turn my head and he's right there wearing a squirrel-squishing grin. I didn't notice him come back in. When did he? I turn stiffly toward the movie and my eyes well up.

Hamish can see every tiny ugly pore of me.

It is a long time before Marc comes back with the drink. When he passes it to me, I say thanks and I hold it up between us for the rest of the stupid movie.

Keep Away

It goes like this.

Marc picks me up at my locker and walks me to class. I pick him up at his class at lunch time. We eat in this classroom in the basement that never gets used. Hamish is there, because he's always there unless Marc tells him to go away, which Marc doesn't like to do too often. I'm helping Marc with his English homework while he holds my hand under the desk.

"That's a soliloquy." I show him Portia's speech.

"Is that Greek for long and boring?" he says.

"They were Romans, Marc. You know, 'Friends, Romans, countrymen…'" He lets go of my hand and flips the book off the desk. It slaps against the floor when it falls.

"What did you do that for?"

"I'm sick of piambic diameter. I don't care anymore. So I fail. So what?"

Hamish smirks at me, then notices Marc giving him the evil eye. He picks the book up and flips through it upside-down, pretending to be interested. Licking his finger and turning the page, nodding at the upside-down print and arching his eyebrows super high on his greasy forehead.

Marc laughs. I so hate Hamish sometimes.

Doesn't he care if his best friend flunks out? He knows better than anyone how gigantically Marc's dad will freak.

"It's not that bad. They're only words. I'll help." I try to get the book out of Hamish's hand, but he throws it over my head to Marc.

They won't let me have it. My foot's better, but it still hurts a little, so I give up trying to get it after the third time.

•

"You are not wearing that," Mom says. I knew I shouldn't have come in the kitchen.

"What? It's a T-shirt and jeans, Mom."

"It's a tight T-shirt — is that Hazel's? — and tight jeans and you look like a teenage prostitute," she says, nudging Dad with the newspaper. He looks up and looks right at my boobs.

"Change," he says. "Now."

He has the meanest look on his face I've ever seen. It's like he's going to hit me.

"All right," I say and walk away from the kitchen. I can hear Mom whisper something behind me. When I get to the bottom of the stairs Dad yells for me to come back. I wipe my eyes and go.

"What?" I scream at them.

Mom comes around the table and hugs me.

"Don't sell yourself short, chickpea," Dad says. "You're a beautiful girl. Doesn't matter what you wear. You make it beautiful. You understand?"

Mom's hugging me hard.

I don't know why I'm crying, but I can't stop.

•

Hazel says, "You have to spend some time away from him because otherwise he'll think he owns you and then he won't be interested anymore."

"Who told you that?"

"Everyone knows that. It's on practically every TV show."

"TV is fiction."

"Yeah, you go on believing that, Glor," she says and goes off to curl her hair with the curling iron she got handed down from Lisa's mother, the pregnant whore.

•

Tina got a part in the school play. She's in drama like Shawna. She's going to be the funny maid. Shawna didn't get a part, but she doesn't seem jealous. If Tina got the part of the girlfriend, then she'd be jealous, but it's okay for Tina to be the maid.

I didn't say anything, but that's what I was thinking.

They're going shopping at Value Village for an apron for Tina's costume. I could have gone, but they didn't even ask me.

I wish I took drama. Then I could hang out with them and wouldn't have to deal with Tizzy looking so revolted by my pictures in art class.

•

Are you allowed to call your boyfriend every day? Hazel says no, but only because she thinks calling a boy at all is whore-y. She gets that from Lisa. I get the feeling, though, that neither of them can wait to be whores. Not real whores, but the calling-boys-on-the-phone kind. Mom should be worrying about the sleazy red shorts Hazel's wearing instead of looking at me every time I go to pick up the phone.

In real life, aren't you supposed to call your boyfriend to show him that you care? It's ten o'clock in the morning already and he hasn't called. He called at nine-thirty last Saturday.

•

Marc and I go for a long walk to celebrate my foot being all better. We walk across the causeway and down by the river near the Royal Military College, holding hands the whole way. Marc shows me how to skip stones until it feels like my arm is going to fall off. Marc tries to hit my stones with his stones. One of Marc's stones skips seven times.

"That's lucky. Seven's lucky," I say, jumping up and down. He has this beaming look on his face and I throw my arms around him. "That was so cool."

"I am lucky," he says, and he eats me up with those Smartie eyes.

I am so in love.

•

Hamish turns out to be a relatively good science partner even though he always pretends to be bad by dropping stuff on the floor. He knows how to write up the results, though, even if he does read them to me in a drone while he bangs his forehead on the desk.

"Why does he act like such an idiot, when it's so

obvious he's intelligent," I ask Marc in the hall between science and geography.

"Because."

"Because why?"

"Because the guy's an idiot, that's why," he says, and I can't help laughing.

Marc pulls his arm tight around my waist and pulls me into the empty auditorium and we make out in the back seats until the bell goes. Marc leaves without even saying goodbye. I watch the door close behind him and have to sit there a couple more minutes because I feel hot in the absolute weirdest way.

When I get to class I exaggerate my leftover limp so that Mr. Linscombe won't send me to the office for a late slip.

•

"He's home. Go." Marc pushes me off the couch. I hear Mr. Le Clare open the fridge upstairs. I fly to the spot under the stairs.

I knew I should have gone. I told him ten minutes ago. But it was already too close to the time when his dad was due home.

I hear Marc start up the video game. He's put a pillow down here for me, because the carpet is sticky.

I feel like Nana's dog, Chi. Nana says, "Go to your place, Chi," and Chi goes and sits on his pillow.

•

"You're coming with us and that's final. You're too young to stay on your own," Dad says. Dad is making us go to Ottawa to visit his friend in the suburbs.

What are they going to do? Force me into the car? I hate Ottawa. I'm not going.

"What are you afraid of, sweetie? You think Marc's going to dump you over the weekend?" Mom says. "Can't he take being without his pookie for two days?"

"Mom. Don't. He's not like that. It's not him. He didn't say anything." I stomp my foot and it hurts so bad I have to sit on the stairs to hold it. But I'm not going to cry. Mom shakes her head, picks up my knapsack and carries it to the car.

"If it's not him, it must be you, then," she says when she comes back for me. "You'll live. I promise."

She holds out her hand to help me up, but I won't give her the satisfaction. I get up and march out the door and don't say a single word for two hours until I absolutely have to ask for a pit stop.

It's not me, either. It's them. It's not my fault if they can't take it that a guy likes me and wants to be with me and wants to kiss me.

After the pit stop, Dad lectures me on sulking until Mom touches his elbow to make him stop. Her doing that makes me angrier than him yapping at me. Then Hazel keeps poking me in the back seat of the car like we're still little kids, doing the I'm-not-touching-you thing.

I sock her in the arm and that breaks the sulk, like she knew it would and I so hate her for making me do it.

We go to the National Gallery where I'm forced to look at bad art — except for the Group of Seven stuff, which is all right and this video art of a woman brushing her hair, which was pretty hysterical until Hazel wouldn't stop imitating it.

In the bathroom before we leave Mom says, "I'm glad we got away. Aren't you? I think it's good to put some air between you and Marc."

And then the whole thing makes sense.

Did they think we would magically stop being in love if I went to Ottawa for the weekend? They think it's just a crush, because we're young.

"Romeo and Juliet were young," I tell Mom when we're back in the car.

"Yeah," she says, "and look what happened to them."

"Only because people wouldn't let them be together."

She can't think of anything to say to that so she just shakes her head. So I win the argument, but I'm still in Ottawa.

•

Sunday night, Hazel does Rapunzel on me. I can hear her breathe in my ear as she brushes my hair back.

"You should brush it a hundred times a night," she says. "You have to take care of yourself, because nobody else will."

"You're taking care of me right now."

"But I'm not always going to be around," she says seriously.

"Why? You going someplace?"

"We'll see," she says. And then it's like she is going away, so I concentrate deeper on her brushing my hair. Seventy-one, seventy-two, seventy-three...

Secret Bosses

Tuesday, between gym and math. Me and Marc are alone outside Exit 5 and he presses me up against the wall and we look in each other's eyes. We kiss with our eyes open so we can see each other while we kiss. I feel him all against me... I wish I could live in this second forever and ever and ever.

•

It happens fast. I hear something on the basement stairs and turn my head in time to meet Marc's dad's eyes. I smile at him. But it's like he doesn't see me even though he's looking straight at me.

"I told you, no girls down here," he says to Marc and points at me, like I don't have ears. Like I was a dog.

"She's helping me, Dad," Marc tells him.

"I bet," says Mr. Le Clare. He goes back upstairs, but it feels like he's still in the room with how charged the air is.

"Did you hear the screen door?" Marc whispers to me and Hamish.

Hamish shakes his head.

"I heard it," I confess. I didn't know Mr. Le Clare would be like that. Parents usually like me.

"Why didn't you go under the stairs?" Marc says, and he slumps on the sofa and waves me away like he's shooing a fly. He won't even look at me.

I don't know what I'm supposed to say, and Hamish is no help at all, as usual. He just shrugs like the whole thing is no big deal.

So I leave.

I have to pass by Mr. Le Clare in the kitchen to get my coat. He's reading a catalogue at the counter. He doesn't look at me. I go out by the back door and walk down the driveway to the front. When I look back at the house I see Mr. Le Clare's face in the living-room window. He sees me and turns his head away, fast.

As soon as I know he can't see me, I start running.

•

On Friday, Marc gives me a stuffed purple puppy-dog key chain. I don't normally go for that stuff, but, you know, my boyfriend gave it to me, so I clip it to my knapsack.

Shawna sees it and goes, "You're changing your whole personality for Marc."

"Yeah. Jealous?"

•

"So why wasn't I invited?" Shawna asks again. She isn't listening.

I turn over on the bed, stuff my pillow under my stomach and switch ears with the phone. This is the third time I've been to the movies with Marc and the third time that Hamish has sat pervertedly right behind us, watching. And Marc won't do anything about it. I've been holding him off by sticking the popcorn between us and he seems all right with that, like popcorn's just as good as kissing. Or maybe he doesn't want Hamish looking, either. So why bring the guy? I want to make out with him at the movies and he doesn't seem to care.

"I am having a problem?" I remind her.

"You can't kiss your boyfriend at the movies. My heart bleeds," she says. "But you get to see the movie. You get to go out and be with people, unlike me, who is not invited. Honestly, I fail to see the problem of the problem."

"I didn't not invite you. I thought we would be alone

this time. Marc said he couldn't wait to be alone with me and that he'd meet me in the park and then I get there and Hamish is there and it was too late to call you."

"There's a phone booth on the corner right there."

"Fine. Next time I'll call. Now can we talk about this? The problem is, he lets Hamish watch." On instinct I look behind me at the hall. Hazel's sitting beside the door listening. I kick the door shut.

"Everything's for him. It's like you're afraid of him. Why didn't you ask him straight out if Hamish was coming? Then you could have called me. But no, it's all about him, like you aren't allowed to know the plan? Why not? You think he doesn't know you don't like having Hamish there? He would tell you the guy was coming if he thought you'd be okay with it. Instead it's all sneaky. I don't like it. You're letting him be the boss of you." Shawna only notices who is the boss because she's used to being the boss.

All that stuff she just said about Marc? Mom's said all that about Shawna.

Shawna may not love that me and Marc are going out, but what she seriously hates is that she doesn't get to be the boss anymore. I don't mind. I like it. Marc is a better boss than Shawna. Except for the video games and Hamish. And not really talking that much. Strike that. That's a good thing. I don't mind not talking. It's peaceful.

"Remember last year when Rachel Pepper and Vanessa went out with Eli, Phil and Gord and Gord's sister?" Shawna asks. "I thought you and me would get a chance to hang out like that before one of us hooked up. That's how it's supposed to work. Tina told me she used to sometimes hang with Serena and Hamish and Marc last year. Only Serena was going out with Marc and they would make out on the couch while she and Hamish played video games. She said it was gross and she didn't know why Serena wanted her there, but she did, but she still stopped going after a while because it was boring and Hamish creeped her out."

"Yeah, I know what she means. Marc is such a good kisser, Shawna," I say. At least we got to kiss on the road on the way home, when Hamish went to the convenience store. I can still see Marc walking backwards away from my front door, the look in his eyes. I had to keep the door mostly closed so Mom couldn't see.

"I know. Not about Marc, but that time I kissed Lawrence – " Here we go. Then Mom walks in with the alarm clock ringing. Saved by the bell.

"I gotta go, Shawna. Mom's got the clock on me."

"My house tomorrow?"

"As usual." I hang up and pass the phone to Mom who takes it but won't stop looking at me.

"What?" I say.

"Nothing. Did you enjoy yourself at the movie?" she asks. Hazel peeks around the door. She doesn't even have the decency to pretend she wasn't sitting out there listening. I bet she already gave Mom a full report.

I roll my eyes.

"When can I have my own room?"

Mom ignores that and takes me by the shoulders, makes me look her in the eye. She arranges my hair over my shoulders and checks my face. I feel myself blush and try to weasel away from her.

"Stop. Still," she instructs, and I hold fast while she looks at my neck. Feeling her Mom hands, her Mom fingers travel the same territory as my boyfriend's.

"No hickeys. But your mouth is really red, pumpkin." She takes my chin in her hand and turns my face toward her, curling her bushy hair behind her ears, which is how she lets us know she means business. "If anything happens, I will know. Do you think you invented smooching at the movies? You didn't invent anything."

"Mom," I say. She kisses my forehead and lets me go.

"Do us all a favor and keep it so we can trust you."

"You're freaking out, Mom," I tell her, and she shakes the phone at me.

"Yeah. Of course I am. I'm not cool with this at all. He's very cute, but I don't know him, and neither do you. You think you do, but you don't. Don't get ahead of yourself or you'll regret it. Getting to know someone is not something you do with your lips."

I sigh big and Mom taps the phone against her cheek, deciding what other obnoxious wisdom to spew on my head. Fortunately, she changes her mind and walks out of the room.

Hazel comes in and parks herself on the end of my bed in her Spiderman boy pajamas. I ignore her and get under the covers with my clothes on. She grabs my feet and knocks them together.

"Ow. Don't. Bad foot," I lie.

"So? Did you guys neck?" she asks. I nod lazily and pull my hair from under my head and let it fan over my pillow. "Did you touch his penis?"

"No. Hazel. Don't ask that." I throw my pillow at her.

"Why not?"

"It's personal."

"I am your sister. You have to tell me everything," she informs me. "You shouldn't go too fast or the boy loses respect and thinks you're a whore. The longer you don't do stuff, the more he wants you to and then you can make him into your slave."

"What about the guy making the girl the slave? That's more what really happens," I say. Her eyes widen in fake shock.

"You're his sex slave? My big sister's a big ho," she says, jumping on me.

"Shhhhh," I warn her and wrestle her into the space between our beds, trying to cover her mouth while she tries to mouth out the word "whore" between tries at biting my hand.

•

Marc hasn't called.

We've already had our eggs and I even ate really slowly to make it go long so that he could call before it was over.

If he's still asleep, I'll kill him.

Okay, I won't kill him. I love him. Ring, phone. Please. What time is it?

I check the clock on the wall and Mom pretends not to notice.

I want him to call me, but I don't want to want that because... isn't a phone call like a present? Isn't a phone call like something you give to someone to let her know you are thinking about her? I don't want him to think that I need him to call. That's so low self-esteem. That's why I should be the one to call him, to show him how generous I can be. But maybe that's the low self-esteem thing to do.

I pick up the phone. Mom looks up from her newspaper and Hazel gives me the evil eye over her Cheerios.

"Don't," she orders, milk dribbling out the side of her mouth. I dial, taking the phone to the dining-room.

"Should I call Marc?" I ask Shawna.

"Does Good Barbie call Ugly Naked?"

"He's not Ugly Naked," I say.

"You don't know that…yet. Don't think about it. Hang up and come over. See you in ten."

"Twenty," I start to say, but she's hung up. My boyfriend doesn't call one morning and she thinks she's boss again.

I go back into the kitchen to put the phone down. Mom and Hazel are staring at me. They heard.

"She meant a Barbie. Ugly Naked is the name of her boy Barbie," I tell them. They nod, completely satisfied with this explanation.

If Marc calls while I'm gone, that's just too bad for him. I'm not the kind of girl who waits by the phone.

I grab my jean jacket and leave before I have time to change my mind. Halfway to Shawna's I remember that Marc's mom is supposedly coming through town today.

If he's with her, then that's okay. I can't be mad about that.

•

The reason I always go to Shawna's is because her house is bigger than mine and she has her own room and a basement rec room and satellite TV. Her parents are never home and even if they are, they stay in the living-room playing with their Palm Pilots and planning where they should buy their fancy cheese. Aside from taking Shawna shopping for clothes and to get her hair cut, Shawna's mother doesn't really notice her or her brother, even though Rod is a bona fide freak who spends most of his time listening to Indian music in his room. Shawna once told me she wishes her family was as close as mine, but first of all, she was lying to make it up to me because she took the last grape popsicle and second, the only reason my family seems so close is because our house is too small.

When I get to Shawna's, we climb into the breakfast nook with Diet Cokes, a piece of paper and a purple magic marker. Shawna wants to make a list of ways to get rid of Hamish so that we can double-date with Marc and some other guy, maybe Joe Grealey from her drama class. Tina told Shawna that he's been to New York and he used to go out with Rosemary, who is the prettiest of the Rideau girls besides Serena. Maybe not him, though, because, Tina told Shawna, he cheated on Rosemary with his own cousin.

"That's disturbing," I tell Shawna.

"Tina says they might be step-cousins and not real cousins," says Shawna. "Better than a squirrel stepper."

"Hamish is Marc's best friend." I don't want Marc to think that I wanted to get rid of his best friend, even though I do want to get rid of him. But what if Marc finds out? Plus, I am all for getting rid of Hamish, but he's the kind of guy who might, I don't know, show up at school with a cross-bow or something.

Over the next couple of hours we come up with:

1. Make Hamish be not Marc's best friend.
2. Make Hamish move to a different city.
3. Get Hamish expelled.
4. Get Hamish a girlfriend.
5. Make Hamish act like a (good) human being.

The last two are in my handwriting. I don't want Shawna thinking too hard about evil ways to get rid of Hamish in case she goes through with one of them and Marc finds out.

Only the top five methods of Hamish neutralization make it onto the sheet. There were many, many more proposed plans, including tying him to a tree at Lemoine Point, taping him into a cardboard box and sticking him

in the middle of the 401, and making him eat roadkill.
Shawna enjoyed that one a little too much. She came up
with recipes. Most of them involved melted cheese.

So, to recap morning with Shawna. Conversation
about Joe Grealey, 2 minutes. Conversation about
Hamish, 2 hours.

I'm beginning to suspect something. I'm working
my way up to asking her about it when the phone rings
and Shawna answers.

"It's for you." She holds out the phone to me and my
heart jumps. Marc is calling me here?

But it's only Mom. She says she wants me to go with
them to look at a condo for Nana. I think she's just
checking up to see if I'm really here and not with Marc.
I've only got ten minutes until they pick me up. I put
the phone down and pick up the piece of paper with
our purple plans on it.

"Who should we try to get to date Hamish?" I ask
Shawna, watching her closely. She starts gathering up
our draft plans and straightening them on the table.

"I think it would be easier to get him expelled," she
says.

"Maybe you should date him," I say. The papers slip
out of her hand and onto the floor. She gets busy picking them up and avoids looking me in the eye.

I rest my case. Boy, oh, boy. Did she have me fooled.

Anything You Want

The condo that we are looking at for Nana is right on the waterfront in front of City Hall. It has a solarium, a garbage disposal and a walk-in closet. It's not on the lake side of the building, but the view is still great and it has two balconies. Dad says Nana can use one of the balconies as her dog-shit balcony.

Mom says Nana wanted us to see this place so we'd have a better picture of the kind of life our parents aren't giving us. She says that after Hazel says the walk-in closet is bigger than Dad's office room.

"You mean the room that's my future bedroom?" I say.

"You wish," Hazel says, and I try to catch Mom's eye, but she won't let me. I'm going to be sharing with Hazel until I get married.

The real estate lady's laugh is so fake that me and

Dad can't take it and have to go out on the balcony to get away from her.

"St. Mary's Cathedral." Dad points at the skyline. "My whole history is in this view. See? Your mom and I got married at the courthouse there. And there's her future: Queen's University. Maybe your future, too. What do you think, chickpea?"

"I think Nana will like it," I say. I wonder where me and Marc will get married? I want an outside wedding. But what if it rains?

"No. I mean, your nana doesn't like anything. But what do you think about going to university? You want to go?" He's looking right in my eyes, so I have to really think.

"I didn't think I was allowed to not want to go." I thought Dad would laugh at that, but he seems serious.

"It's your life, Gloria," he says. "You can do whatever you want with it. Whatever you want, that's what we want for you."

He kisses me on the head, like he's saying goodbye forever. Then he leaves me there, on Nana's future dog-shit balcony. I hear the click of the sliding door like it's something out of a movie where the girl suddenly feels like she's all alone in her new apartment and every single thing in her life is all up to her. And it makes her feel full and empty at the same time.

And I'm the girl.

My mind goes back to last Tuesday when me and Marc kissed out back of Exit 5 and I wanted to stay there forever and live with his arms around my waist and his eyes locked on my eyes.

Dad pokes his head out the balcony doors.

"You don't have to figure out your whole future right now," he says. "We're going across the street for ice cream."

•

I'm in the bathtub while everyone else watches TV downstairs. I'm trying to think about the Exit 5 kiss again, but it's hard to concentrate with the drippy faucet and the fake laughing on the TV.

I'm pruning up and the bath water is getting cold. I let some water out and fill up the tub with hot again. Five more minutes and then I'm calling Marc.

When we got home from Nana's condo I checked for messages. Marc had called to say he was on his way to meet his mom up at Pizza Hut. I knew it. It's good they worked it out. He was worried. His eyes squint when he's worried. I just want to grab his head and kiss it all over to take away the sadness. Only he doesn't like me to touch him when he's being sad.

Marc's mom shouldn't treat him like that. She

should come into town. Who cares what her boyfriend thinks? Anyone knows the son is more important than the stupid boyfriend. I'd never have a boyfriend who wouldn't let me see my kid. Poor Marc.

I should have stayed home today in case he needed me. I should have called him this morning. It was a huge day for him, and I was worried what it would look like if I called?

I wish there was a rule book somewhere on how to be a girlfriend. I wish I could flip to the index and find "boyfriend's mother" or "calling weekend mornings" or "total future management."

I sink lower into the water and turn on my side to submerge my uncovered parts. Some water sloshes over the side.

I imagine what our kids will look like. A boy and a girl. They both look like him, which is a little too bad for the girl. I rub out their faces and switch them to being babies. One baby. I put our family in the solarium of Nana's new condo. I'm reading in an imaginary rocking chair while my baby boy plays with blocks beside me. Marc's in the kitchen making a sandwich… with Hamish. I click on Hamish with my brain mouse and hit my mental Delete button.

I add more hot water to the tub and roll over to change fantasy channels.

"Gloria Le Clare," I whisper to the side of the tub.

Me and Marc could live in a house like Shawna's and read magazines in her parents' king-sized bed with the gold bedspread. Marc reaches for the remote for the satellite TV. No. Scratch that. Turn off the TV. We are necking and I am in a long white satin negligee, like the one Good Barbie wears when she is saying no to Ugly Naked. Only I will not say no to my husband, Marc, and he'll pull the negligee off over my head.

Better turn off the lights.

There.

We are naked and our whole skins are rubbing against each other's whole skins. He is kissing me on my neck and all over, and I am kissing him back and holding him tight so that I can feel his stomach breathe out against my stomach. His hands are on my back, pressing...

"Hurry up, I gotta pee." Hazel knocks on the door.

"Go away," I yell, slapping the bath water.

If only I had my own room.

•

When I call, the phone picks up on the third ring and the voice says, "Marc?"

"Hello, Mr. Le Clare," I say.

"Who's this?"

"It's Gloria. I guess Marc isn't there."

"You're the tutor?"

"Yes," I lie.

"You see Marc today?" he asks.

He didn't tell his dad about meeting his mom at Pizza Hut.

"No," I say truthfully. "I was out with my family." Why did I say that? I shouldn't have called. I should have waited for Marc to call me. If only I was here this afternoon when he called, then Dad could have driven him.

"Oh. If you see him, tell him to come home. Or call." He hangs up.

I stay downstairs after eleven waiting for Marc to call. It's quiet down here when my family's in bed. Except for the fridge, which hums so loud I want to kick it. Then even it kicks off and the only sound left is the clicking of the eyes of the cat clock going back and forth.

Baby Owls

I was going to walk to school today, but Dad decided he was going to drive me on his way to this meeting and then he kept saying "two more minutes" and wouldn't get off the computer. He's all hyper about this government contract he bid on. Anyway, I could have walked and now I'm late for school and won't get a chance to hold hands with Marc on our way to science class.

I slam the car door behind me to show how angry I am. Dad honks the horn and makes me look back.

"Who loves you, baby?" he waves, grinning, like he knows exactly what he's ruined for me.

By the time I get to class everyone is already working on their experiments, but I don't see Marc.

"Where's Marc?" I ask Hamish.

"Maybe it didn't go so well with Mummykins. Or maybe, maybe, he went with her to Ottawa. Or, maybe

168

he's going to move to Toronto with her. Boo-hoo for you." Hamish rubs fake tears off his cheeks.

How can Shawna possibly like him?

"He said he couldn't move to Toronto because he had to look after you," I say. Hamish straightens up and gets out his binder.

"Him take care of me? Ha. That's funny," he says, looking out the window and strumming his pen against his teeth. He narrows his eyes at me. "You don't think I take care of him? Do I not bring his girlfriend Coca-Cola? Do I not help him cheat on tests?"

He is such a liar. Marc does not cheat. His marks are bad. Cheaters get good marks.

"You stepped on a dead squirrel," I burst. The kids at the desks around us go quiet. They're looking at me. "Tina told me. On the road? Last spring?"

"Oh, yeah," he says, remembering. "And that's relevant because?"

"Let's just do the experiment. Get it over with." And I grab the beaker and go to get some water.

When we are writing up the results, I catch him looking toward the back of the class for Marc.

"So?" he says, embarrassed. I don't say anything. He turns in his seat to face me. "What if I told you he paid me five dollars to step on the squirrel?"

I look at him. I can't tell if he's lying or not.

"Marc wouldn't do that," I say.

"Sure. You go on thinking that," he says, and the bell rings.

•

I am watching Tizzy start on a contour drawing of baby owls. His hand knows exactly where it needs to go to make the owls be babies. His hand knows where the baby owl eyes are and how the baby owl legs go on the branch of the tree. He makes it so you know it's a tree branch without him having to draw the tree. It's like the whole picture was stored in his pencil and all he had to do was move his hand across the page.

I am drawing a picture of my room, or what it would look like if I had a room. It looks like crap. I've erased the bed three times already. I blow eraser shavings off my page and they go onto Tiz's picture. He looks up at me.

"Sorry. Your owls look good. Are they for your grandmother, too?"

He shakes his head and brings his hairy face closer to the picture to work on the feathers, which I can tell is going to take him a long time. He doesn't talk to me as much as he used to. I know it's because he likes me a little and he's mad about Marc. I don't want it to be like this all year.

"Is she feeling better now?" I ask.

"Why do you care?" he snaps.

"I was just asking." I return to working on my crappy picture. I can't believe I made it worse instead of better.

After a while Tizzy clears his throat.

"You should be careful of Marc. Okay, there, I finally said it. My grandmother's fine, thank you for asking. And you shouldn't hold your pencil like that so close to the end. Try it further up. You're so messy, it drives me nuts."

I'm so relieved that he broke the tension that I start laughing and then, when I finally get myself under control, it feels too dangerous to ask what he means about Marc.

He's probably just jealous, right? Then like he's reading my mind, he lifts his head from his baby owls and looks me straight in the eye.

"I'm not saying he's a bad guy. Just be careful. That's all I'm saying." He waits for me to nod, which I do. Then his head drops back to the feathers of the owls. "You could do better," he says, still looking at the page. "That's all I'm saying."

•

What's different this year? Why do boys like me now?

It's because my boobs got big. But I don't want that. I don't want it to be like that. I don't want to be a pair of flesh balls walking down the hall.

•

Shawna is talking about how people should be whipped for tucking sweaters into jeans. She is, of course, making fun of Rachel Pepper, who is wearing a fuzzy magenta sweater, which she has tucked into her jeans so she can show off the cool silver buckle on her belt.

"She doesn't have a waist, so she is inventing one. I'd almost admire her if it weren't for the tucking-in-the-sweater thing. It's so counter-productive. I mean, why bother trying to invent a waist that's all bulked up by sweater?" She's asking Tina, who is the worst of the fashion victims, but at least she isn't wearing the wrong pants anymore. I wonder if Shawna clued her in about those?

Tina isn't eating at all today. Instead, she has almost a whole pack of sugarless cinnamon gum in her mouth.

Shawna's been pretending not to notice that Marc isn't here, so I've been testing how long she'll last without saying anything about it.

"So you're eating with us today," she says. I nod. "How come?"

"I don't know where Marc is. He went to meet his mom yesterday. I asked Hamish about him in science, but he hasn't heard anything, either." Shawna and Tina absorb this information. "Hamish said that Marc paid him to step on the squirrel. He's lying, right, Tina?"

"Wow," says Shawna, buying it a little too quickly. I shouldn't have said anything. I should have asked Marc about it first.

"I don't know," Tina says. "I have to think." She sits up in her chair and rubs her arms. She looks at me. "What do you think? Do you think Marc would do that?"

She knows something.

"He's my boyfriend," I say. Tina bites her lip and we try to figure it out in the air between our faces. Shawna can't take it.

"Guys. It was a dead squirrel. It wasn't like hurting a person or a live squirrel. Even if it's true, is it really that big a deal?"

"Your roadkill crush is showing," I snap at her.

"Roadkill crush," Tina repeats. "You are so right on with that, girly."

For the rest of lunch we tease Shawna mercilessly about her crush on Hamish. How did I not see it before yesterday? She was so burnt up when she found out he was my science partner. She wanted to meet him outside Exit 5. Sure she said it was about trying to hook up with Marc. Wait, did she even say that?

Shawna tells me to shut up with every new piece of

evidence I dig up on her roadkill crush. Then Tina admits that she and Shawna crank-called Hamish's house the night Tina slept over.

"Shawna said she wanted to see if Hamish left you and Marc alone. Then Hamish answers the phone and Shawna goes, 'Lo, lo, lo, lo, lo, lo, lo.'"

"What's that supposed to be?" I ask Shawna, who is blushing so hard that her ears are almost purple.

"I didn't know what to say. So I lo-ed," she says.

Then we all try it.

Nothing is more fun than lo-ing with your two best friends in the cafeteria. I highly recommend it.

Coming Up and Out

Between gym and geography, Tina finds me in the hall. She pulls on my sleeve and leads me into the washroom by the third-floor teachers' lounge.

"What?" I ask her. But she puts her finger to her lips and looks under the doors of the yellow stalls. When she stands up to face me, she's not smiling. She comes over to the window and hoists herself up onto the broad windowsill. She leans her face against the glass, makes fog on the window with her breath and runs her finger through it.

I'm waiting.

"So?" I ask.

"There's something I have to tell you but you have to swear you won't tell Shawna." She sounds so serious.

"What is it?" I ask.

"You won't tell Shawna?"

"Does it have something to do with her? Because if it does, I can't promise not to tell her." My arms feel cold and I step closer to the window to feel the sun.

"It doesn't. It might. Maybe this isn't a good idea." She jumps down from the window and I stop her from going for the door.

"Wait." She takes a step back. She's holding her breath. "Okay, I won't tell."

She looks me in the eye and leans sideways against the wall and runs her finger along the edge of the molding, concentrating on the tip of a piece of insulation that's sticking through. I watch her pull at it.

"You need to know about this and that's the only reason I'm telling you." She checks my face. I hold still. "You remember when you asked me why I don't hang out with any of the girls from my old school?"

I nod. She turns to look at the piece of fluff.

"It's because they think I'm gay."

I don't know what to say. I haven't heard any of the Rideau girls say anything like that. Although, come to think of it, Hamish did say that about Shawna and Tina being girlfriends. Oh.

"I used to be best friends with Serena. The one who went out with Marc? She moved out west?"

"I know who Serena is," I say. "I know about you guys."

"What? What do you know?" Tina snaps.

"Just that you guys used to play video games in Marc's basement while Marc and Serena made out."

Tina nods. What is this? She talks about Serena all the time. I didn't mind because I was curious. I wanted to know what other kind of girl Marc had picked. Was she like me? I asked him, but he just goes "no" and laughs and then looks at Hamish.

Tina told me and Shawna that Serena wore a lot of white, like white jeans and white T-shirts and a white ski-vest in winter. And she was skinny and she was smart, but not as smart as me or Shawna. And she once saw Serena take money from her grandma's wallet so that they could go to the movies.

"The Rideau girls thought you and Serena were girl-friends? Was that what you had to tell me?" I ask. "But she was going out with Marc. No offense, but some of those Rideau girls are dumb as stumps. Man, a girl can't even have a best friend anymore."

Tina's still holding her breath. The halls outside are going quiet. I have to get to class. I adjust my knapsack on my back and turn to go.

"I'm just trying to figure how to say this. Hamish… no…Marc… I don't know which one, but one of them paid Serena to kiss me."

"What?" My knapsack slides off my shoulder and onto the ground with a thud.

"We were in Marc's basement and I was coming out of the washroom and Serena pushed me back in. She said she wanted to try a new hairstyle on me. She said she was bored and that we were going to do a fashion show for the boys. So I sat on the toilet and she did my hair in a French braid. Then I did her hair — her hair was so blonde it was almost white and straight — in a bun. And she yells out the door, 'Almost ready, guys.' Then she's doing last touch-ups on my hair and she stands really, really close and I'm looking up at her. She was tall. And she pushes me up against the wall and she kisses me right on the mouth. I didn't know what she was doing, so I went along with it. When we stopped, the bathroom door was wide open and Marc and Hamish were right there. Then she puts her hand out and tells them, 'Pay up.' I always thought it was Hamish, because he's so, you know… But it was Marc who gave her the money. Twenty dollars. Then Hamish told everyone he saw me kiss Serena. Of course they didn't think she was the one who was gay. People don't think that about pretty girls."

"But if she forced you then it's not your fault. It wasn't your idea." Marc paid his girlfriend to kiss her friend? "It must have been Hamish's idea. Marc wouldn't do that," I tell her. She shrugs, like she's agreeing, but I can tell she's not.

178

"I didn't think so either, until today. But he was there, right? And he was the one who gave her the money. And he must've been the one she told, because she wouldn't have told that to Hamish," Tina says.

I'm lost.

"What wouldn't she have told to Hamish?"

Tina takes a deep breath and aims her eyes at the ceiling.

"It wasn't the first time me and her kissed. She must've told him."

I stumble back against the wall.

"Please, please don't tell Shawna," Tina begs me. "I had to tell you. You had to know that Marc...he seems nice, but he might trick you or something. He might make you do something." She's panicking now.

I don't believe it. I do, but I don't. I can't.

Her face is red and tight. She looks at her watch. I remember Marc's lips, and about him being a fast artist. He and Hamish disappearing and coming back stoned. And the movie theater with Hamish sitting behind us. The smell of spilled Coke when I hide under the stairs. Marc lying to his dad. His hands pressing on my back. Tizzy saying, "You should be careful of Marc."

Marc's lips.

"We should go. I'll call you tonight," Tina says. She

starts for the door and then stops. "Don't you want to know if it's true?"

"What?" It takes me a moment to focus back on her.

"Don't you want to know if I'm gay?" she blurts.

"Are you?"

"I used to be, with Serena. But I don't think I am anymore. I mean, I still think Marc is ultra hot," she answers, but it sounds fake. Not like she's lying, but like she's saying it for me.

She's saying that about Marc in case I keep seeing him. In case. She just told me the biggest secret of her life.

I adjust my knapsack strap on my shoulder. Tina waits.

"You promised you wouldn't tell Shawna, remember. I'm going to tell her. I just wanted for her to like me first. As a friend." She makes for the door and I grab her by the back of her pants. "What?" she snaps. I let her go and she pulls open the door.

"Tina," I say. She turns around, finally. "That time you told us about when you were kissing in the garage when you were playing Sardines? That was with Serena, right?"

Tina throws her head back to keep the tears from falling down her cheeks.

"Yes," she says. She screws up her mouth and leaves, wiping her eyes.

•

I don't even remember how I got to geography class. Some girl is going on about the Amazon rainforest and all I can think about is Marc pulling money out of the monkey head to pay off Serena for kissing Tina.

I wipe my eyes. Mr. Linscombe is looking at me.

He asks me if there's a problem and I shake my head, but as I do I feel my face screw up.

"Maybe you need to go to the guidance office?" he asks. I shrug and he waves his hand for me to go. So then I have to go.

I have to sit in the waiting room while the guidance counselor deals with some other girl. I can hear the girl crying through the door. I'm crying, too. But not as hard.

I stop to listen.

Whatever is wrong with that girl is deeply wrong. And the guidance counselor goes, "Shh, shh, shh."

I pick up my books and leave the waiting room. I let myself into the empty auditorium and sit in the back row. The stage is far, far away. It looks small and dark.

I imagine Marc's basement couch in the middle of it with Hamish's stool set off to one side and the TV in the center of the stage. There I am on the left, with my legs over Marc's lap and we are kissing and Hamish is playing video games. A slit of light beams through the closed door on the right. That's the washroom. Someone's in there hiding, just like I've hidden. There are the stairs and the foggy black darkness underneath them. Another hiding spot, for who? Serena will come out of there, like a tall ghost in super-tight white jeans and with her almost-white blonde hair streaming behind her in a blur. That will be my cue to scream and I will scream into Marc's mouth and Hamish will start laughing as the door opens.

I really don't feel so good here in the dark.

That girl, the one in the guidance office? I bet she was pregnant.

●

After school, Hamish comes by my locker.

"Marc wants to see you," he says. My heart squirms a little, but I tell it to stay still.

"Where is he?" I ask. Tina and Shawna are coming down the hall. We both see them.

"He said to meet him at his house," Hamish says quickly. He wants to take off before the girls get here.

"Why didn't he come to school today?"

"He just felt like blowing it off." He starts down the hall.

"Did you go to his place at lunch?" I call after him,

but he just keeps on moving. Shawna stares down the hall after Hamish and slumps against the locker beside mine.

"It's like he's allergic to me," she says. Now that we've uncovered her crush she's going to talk non-stop about it until we hook her up with Hamish and then she'll talk non-stop about that and then…

Now that I think about it, there is no way to stop the world from revolving around Shawna.

"You want to come over?"

"I wish I could, but I have to go to Marc's."

"You wish you could? Liar. Kissy-kissy mmmmmm," she says.

"It's not all like that," I tell her.

If she only knew. First I have to watch video games. Then I have to try a video game to pretend I'm interested. Then at around five Hamish goes. Then kissy-kissy until 5:15 and leave before Marc's dad gets home, or hide under the stairs and make a run for it when Mr. Le Clare goes to the upstairs washroom. Once he stayed downstairs with Marc to watch TV and left the door open when he went to the downstairs washroom. I had to run past him to get out of there before Mom called.

"Believe me. It's not all making out."

"Sure, sure. You have to talk sometimes to make like

you're interested in each other's minds. What beautiful picture-perfect minds you both have."

"You know I have a mind," I protest.

"Yeah, and I'm sure your mind is just as important to Marc as the other parts of you," she says, staring pointedly at my chest.

"Shawna!" Tina smacks her arm.

"What? She knows I'm joking."

"It doesn't feel like a joke," Tina says. Shawna gogs her eyes out, like we're the ones acting up.

"I don't know, Tina. If minds don't really matter, that means she must be hot for Hamish's bod," I tease, and Shawna blushes so hard. I've never seen her like this. She's completely adorable when she's embarrassed. Even her ears are burning red. I can't help laughing.

"You've got it bad, girl," Tina tells her.

"Shut up, you guys," Shawna says, happy enough to have the spotlight back on her.

They walk with me to the corner and I turn off for Marc's place. It's strange coming here on my own. It doesn't feel right. I feel like someone is going to come out onto a porch and ask me where I think I'm going.

When I ring the bell, Marc comes to the door barefoot in ripped jean shorts and a sleeveless orange T-shirt. His dark hair is all tousled and he's got a crease in the side of his face.

"Were you sleeping?" I ask. He nods and opens the door, digging sleep out of the side of his eye. "How did it go with your mom?"

"She came. We ate. She left. She's going to have another kid."

My mind goes to Hazel's friend Lisa calling her mother a whore for getting pregnant by her boyfriend. I try to see Marc's eyes but he's walking down the hall now and running down the basement stairs. By the time I get down there, he's already playing a video game.

I sit beside him and wait. The game goes on for four minutes and then ends. I think now he's going to talk to me, but he just resets the game.

About halfway through the second game, I can't take it anymore.

"Hamish said you wanted to see me?"

"Yeah, so?" Meep, blast, squeal, crash.

"So what did you want to see me about?" He plays another minute and then puts the thing on Pause.

"I thought you would at least call me when I didn't show up at school," he says, pushing the controls onto the floor.

"I didn't know you wanted me to," I say. My head is spinning.

"You could have called me yesterday," he says.

185

"I did, but you were out."

"After, I mean."

"You could have called me, too. I waited for you to call," I say, getting angry. He stares at me, his eyes small and sharp. I shrink into the couch. "I'm sorry about your mom, Marc."

He stomps on the video game control panel with his heel. It doesn't break. I feel waves of mad coming off him and it makes the room feel hot and cold at the same time, like a fever. I look underneath the stairs so I don't have to look at Marc.

I hate it down here.

"You should see my dad. He's totally burnt. Mom's ruining his life."

"I thought your dad was seeing someone?" I say. He sits back and stares at me, shaking his head.

"You don't get anything. I told you, he never brings his girls home. He doesn't like them like that. Don't you get that? I thought you were supposed to be smart. I brought you home, see?" He shakes his head at me and crosses his arms. "Biggest mistake of my life."

My heart falls out of my chest. I'm stuck here with my arms at my sides, dying.

I make a move toward him and he tightens his arms against his chest.

"Marc?" He turns his head away from me. "You

brought Serena here." I look again at the dark spot under the stairs.

"Well, she's not here anymore," he says, like it's my fault.

This is because of his mom. As soon as I get it, I pick my heart up off the floor and turn to face him.

"I'm really sorry I didn't call. I didn't know you'd want me to. Next time I will, okay?"

"There better not be a next time or I'll kill him," he says, staring at the TV.

"Who?"

"My mom's boyfriend, that's who. She and my dad aren't even divorced yet and she's going to have kids with this guy. Now she's never going to come. She wasn't even going to order a dessert. She said she was tired. Too tired for a fucking piece of cake?" He spits the last word. I can see him up there at Pizza Hut sipping on his Coke trying to convince his mom to stay for cake.

"I'm so sorry, Marc," I say and put my hand on his back. "I'm so sorry she's being like that. You deserve better."

"It's his fault," he says and looks at me. His eyes are still angry, but they are wet on the sides. He looks down when he sees me see his eyes.

His lower lip sticks out and he lets his head fall in his hands.

I rub his back and he turns in toward me, raising his mouth to meet mine. I can feel the tears on his cheeks as we kiss and the wet of them squeezes between our lips and the salt of them leaks into us.

I am so, so sorry. If only I had called. He's my boyfriend.

I taste his tears and hold his face in my hands and draw him closer. We stop kissing and we hug and like the guidance counselor with the crying girl, I say, "Shh, shh, shh."

I hear the low buzz of the stalled TV screen and the hum of the fridge upstairs. The basement dims as the sun lowers in the sky outside, making the room feel like it is closing in on us.

I squeeze him tighter and feel the weight of him against me. He is curled up, like a little boy. I kiss his neck and send some closed-eye warmth his way.

"It's okay," I whisper and he presses against me.

He pushes me under him on the couch until he is lying on top of me. He wraps his arms around my neck and lies still. I like the weight of him on me. I feel tucked in, and I lean my head against his arm to look at him, but I can only see the top of his head.

"Are you all right?" I ask. It's a little hard to breathe.

He doesn't answer, but begins kissing my face all over

— wet and sloppy puppy kisses. His eyes are closed.

"Marc," I giggle, but he doesn't stop and he's moving too fast. I can hear his breath in my ear in short, tight grunts.

I try to catch his face with my hands. But he takes my wrists and pins them over my head, pressing his hips hard into mine and grinding against me. I try to move my arms but he holds them fast and still won't open his eyes. I duck my head to get it away from his mouth, but he keeps going.

An alarm goes off inside me. Not this.

"Stop. Marc? Please." Grind. Grind. Grind. *"No,"* I yell and knee him in the groin. I hear a quick suck of air by my head and he slumps on top of me. I push him off, let myself fall on the floor and shakily stand up. I balance myself against the TV set and look at him curled on the couch.

He looks like a stranger.

How did I get here? I look at the dark space under the stairs. Did Serena let him do that?

"Why did you do that?" I ask. I want to know. I want to know the real reason.

"I didn't know you didn't want me to," he says, sitting up and tossing his hair to the side.

"I didn't." I'm still shaking.

"So? How was I supposed to know? Don't be like

that. Come on. Relax," he says, activating his dimples. "Come on, sit down."

I go off. I mentally tunnel into his deepest dimple and try to poke it out of his cheek like the eye of a potato. My body is coursing with needles and zoom. I feel screams come ready in my mouth and take a deep breath to shove them down.

"Don't be like what? What should I be like, Marc? Should I just go along with anything you want? Is that what you want, for me to just lie there and take it?"

"I thought you'd like it. I know you like everything else," he says, grinning.

He looks at me and the look is proud and hard and cold — and it doesn't see me. He blinks, shrugs and looks past me to the TV, picks up the video controls and resets his game. I wait a few seconds and then I don't know what I'm waiting for.

I hate his face now.

His beautiful face. I feel my eyes start to fill.

I run upstairs and stop at the top to hear if he's coming. No. He's not going to come.

I go out the back door and remember kissing him in the driveway that day he double-rode me home on his bike. I put my hand over my mouth and look at the closed door.

He could still come. It's not too late.

But the door doesn't move. I wipe my nose with the sleeve of my jacket and start moving down the driveway.

He was just a cute boy, that's all. It's not like we were going to get married.

He thought he could have any girl because that's what he was used to. And so he thought he could have me and do whatever. But I'm not like that. I don't want it if it's going to be that way.

Hamish is sitting on Marc's porch looking at a store flyer. He looks up at me as I come down the driveway. He checks out my face. I expect his cruel grin, but get a look of sympathy instead.

"What happened?" he asks and comes down to meet me.

"Nothing. It's stupid."

"What kind of stupid?" But I can tell, Hamish knows exactly what kind of stupid. What a pair of sickos.

I try to keep my face straight by looking down the street toward the phone booth by the convenience store.

"I need to call my dad to pick me up. You got a quarter?"

He searches around in his pocket and comes out with two dimes and a nickel.

"Thanks," I say. Hamish looks down at his feet.

"Why did you tell everyone about Tina and Serena?" I ask him. He looks up and smirks.

"Maybe that's what she gets for not putting out," Hamish says, though I see how fast he looks away.

Okay, so that's it. Guys are pigs. I stand up to leave.

"Pig," I say and cross the street to call Dad. I sit on the curb to wait. Hamish has gone back to sitting on Marc's front steps, hitting the rolled-up flyer against his knees, waiting for Marc to come out and get him.

He keeps looking my way.

Why doesn't he go inside to his pig master?

•

As soon as I'm in the car Dad says, "So?"

"We broke up," I tell him. I hate the huge smile that blooms on his face.

"What'd he do?"

"Nothing. Don't make me talk about it," I say, my voice catching at the end.

Dad goes silent for a while and stops grinning, but keeps trying to look at my face. I turn away from him and watch the falling leaves above Johnson Street and sniff the sweaty-sock smell of our car and try to keep from crying.

"He did something, didn't he? I'm going to kill him." Dad bangs the steering wheel with his hand and we veer left. I hold on to the dash as he gets the car back on track. We stop at the next corner. The look on his face — I can't help laughing, even though I'm still half-crying. His eyes are all bugged out, his face is red and his jaw's hanging loose.

"What?" he says. Then we're both quiet until we pull into the driveway. Dad takes the key out of the ignition and sits, waiting for me.

"Don't worry about it, Dad. I handled it. Okay?" I search his face.

"Okay," he says, finally.

I go to the living-room and Dad goes to the kitchen where I hear him tell Mom, "She fired her boyfriend."

And Mom says, "Thank God."

•

The orange piece of paper says: Gloria and Marc. Marc and Gloria. Mrs. Marc Le Clare. Mr. and Mrs. Marc Le Clare. Mrs. Le Clare. Mrs. Gloria Le Clare. Dr. Gloria Le Clare. Dr. Le Clare-Nunes. Ms. Gloria Le Clare. Ms. Le Clare. I rip it up into tiny pieces, then hold the pieces in my hand while I wait for the bathroom to come free, so I can flush the pieces down the toilet.

I am Gloria Nunes. That's who I always will be. For better or for worse. For richer or for poorer. In sickness and in health. In school and at home.

With boyfriend or without.

•

Hazel asks, "So who'd he dump you for?"

I tell her that I dumped him and she says, "I'm glad you dumped him. That means you're the winner."

•

Shawna can't believe that me and Marc are broken up. Mostly I bet she can't believe it because she still wants Hamish and can't give up the dream of us double-dating. I'm pacing the front hall with the phone. Mom and Hazel are watching TV and Dad's upstairs clacking away on the computer.

"Maybe he just, like, wanted you?"

"No, Shawna. You weren't there. That's not it."

"So you're the expert now?"

"Yes, I am." I hear her breathing on the other end of the phone. She doesn't want me to know more than her about stuff like this. Too bad. I wish I wasn't an expert, but it happened to me and it can't unhappen.

"But he was a true boyfriend, Glor. I know. I saw," she says, and my stomach twinges. "What if he apologizes? Then will you get back together?"

I think about it. I know Marc was a true boyfriend, but — it wasn't right. I wanted it to be right, but it wasn't. And now…it's not like I don't think about him, about everything. But it's different.

"Why do you want us to get back together so badly?"

"I thought he made you happy."

"Marc wasn't what I wanted, Shawna. He's what I accidentally got."

"Okay. I heard you," Shawna says. "I'm sorry it didn't work out. Really I am. It's only too bad because Tina told me that Marc has a cousin who visits from Toronto sometimes, and he's supposed to be cute, like, cuter than Marc. But he's almost eighteen, and it's not like he lives in town. So…" She lets it dangle.

So that's it.

"But what about your roadkill crush?" I say.

"I can't be into Hamish after what Tina told me."

"Tina told you?"

"About him and Marc paying Serena to kiss her, and about Serena and Tina making out once before that. Yeah. Rosemary already warned me about Tina. Can you believe that? As if I'd blow Tina off when she's the only girl from Rideau who shows any originality whatsoever."

"I like Tina," I say, nodding into the phone.

"Yeah, she's weird. In a good way."

I take a bite of my apple and throw my leg over the kitchen table. I look at my reflection in the glass of the deck doors and adjust my Catwoman T-shirt.

"Hey, Shawna, do I seem taller to you?"

Autumn Equinox

Shawna has me and Tina sleep over to celebrate her fourteen-and-a-half birthday. Shawna created the half birthday so that she could have more days in the year that were totally about her. She even made her own half-moon birthday cake with blue icing decorated with gold stars. Tina has had three pieces with extra icing and says she isn't going to eat tomorrow. But Shawna says she has a plan for Tina to burn off the cake.

She takes us up to her room and shows us the three boats she got her brother, Rod, to make her out of newspaper. He's into yoga and origami and burns incense and stuff. We're supposed to put our wishes for the year in the paper boats, set them on fire and launch them in the lake. Shawna says it's an autumn equinox thing. Of course, Shawna's half birthday is in the middle of October which is way after the autumn equinox, but when I try to correct her on it, she rolls her eyes at me, like I'm the one who's crazy.

We start painting the boats and Shawna gets the idea to put the Barbies in them to commemorate "the end of childhood."

"I thought this was an autumn equinox, half-birthday thing?" I say. I don't want to burn the Barbies.

"It is. It's about saying goodbye to the light — like daylight, because it's going to be dark now, and like childhood, because adulthood is darker than child-hood."

I think Shawna's just looking for an excuse to burn Barbies. Tina rolls her eyes. Shawna passes her Ugly Naked and says, "Just pretend it's Serena."

"You want me to burn my best friend?" Tina says.

"Ex-friend," corrects Shawna.

She hands me Second Good, as usual.

"I'm not burning her. I don't want to burn my child-hood."

"Fine. Don't. But I'm burning Good," she says.

"At least let me keep the gold dress," I say, tearing it out of her hand. She doesn't want me to have it, but in the end she lets me keep it. She doesn't want to look too petty in front of Tina, who doesn't understand the his-torical importance of the gold dress.

When Shawna goes to the washroom I put Leggy, the plastic leg boyfriend, in my knapsack.

We make lists of wishes to put on our paper boats. Shawna wishes for an end to world poverty, to grow four inches (in height), to meet a beautiful, funny, rich boy who "gets" her or for Joe Grealey to ask her to the Halloween Dance. Tina wishes for world peace, to lose seven pounds to fit into this red dress she bought last year, and to fall in love with someone who loves her for who she is.

I say my wish is for everyone else's wishes to come true. Shawna says that's a cop-out. I say that it's all I'm wishing for and she'll just have to accept it. She doesn't remember, but I do, the last time I made a wish with her.

You have to be careful with wishes. You have to be ready for if they come true.

We wait until eleven-thirty at night, then sneak out and take our paper boats down to the pier below King Street.

It's quiet down by the water and so beautiful with the sound of the waves shushing against the rocks.

I do have one thing I could wish for.

I pull Second Good out of my pocket and sit her in my boat beside me.

When Tina's watch reads midnight, we get down on

our stomachs, put the boats in the water and light them on fire.

Then we dangle our legs over the side of the pier, silently watching our wish boats burn in the cool autumn night.

Sarah Withrow is the author of *The Black Sunshine of Goody Pryne*, *Box Girl* and *Bat Summer*, which was nominated for a Governor General's award and has been published in seven countries. She also works as a communications officer at Queen's University in the eastern Ontario city of Kingston — the setting for most of her novels.